Legacy

Book 1 of Expanding Suns (TM)

David Aquinas

David Aquinas Publishing

CONTENTS

1

A WRINKLE IN SPACE-TIME

In the 50th year since the ascendance of paramani Kashendra Ashastra to the Emerald Dais to rule all humans, there arose a disturbance in deep space core ward at the heart of the Commonwealth of Stars. A virtual wind sprang deep in the ether between the continuums of n-space. It surged like an unseasonable storm in the climate of ever turning spheres of reality that made up the cosmos. It ripped through the layers of space-time, attracted and repelled by anchoring gravity wells, resonating with the hidden mirrors that sparkled like evanescent jewels with colors ephemeral and eternal, unbeheld by sapient eyes of any aliens in the Commonwealth.

A saren philosopher might blame the lowly humans; newcomers deemed primitive and irrelevant, yet they seemed to attract waves of discontinuity, pulsing between infinite potential and eternal stasis, the human enigma whose gift was unknown, but always seemed to draw trouble unto itself.

Now, the cosmic wind shook the webwork of reality called space-time, and a merchant ship of one of the noble houses of the human worlds, whose people called themselves the Altari, shuddered as tendrils of gravity waves probed its hull.

The bridge crew at station tried to hold the ship on course, but something had gone drastically wrong for the merchant ship *Castellan*. Her captain, Jolanda ni Demarest, should not have taken a route so deep into n-space. Bad things happened pushing transit speeds so hard, but House Zayan had paid a triple bounty for a shipment of gravity impellers and fusion packs,and other goods illegally redacted from the manifest in return for personal considerations.

Captain Demarest had almost turned down the job, but everyone in the Altari Republic strove for wealth and status, and she ignored Zayan machinations, to gather a few more gold quants into her pension fund.

She wondered if Zayans were really human at all, but they always paid well,and she had been hoping for one more run before retiring.

The bridge, compact, had stations for three others and she called on them now. "Tac-O why have webeen forced out of jump?"

The tactical officer,a junior son of a minor house family, worked the board, hesitating, then inhaste answered. "A gravity wave anomaly has disrupted the jump lane."

Felgercarb. She pushed the curse word away, fear rising. "Comm-O, any friendly signals nearby?"

The communications officer, a House Santander seventh daughter, answered. "No depot signals of anykind."

The captain would have welcomed even pirates rather than fall into uncharted space. "Nav-O, are there any nexus points mapped or unmapped within range?"

A willowy, tall woman, a commoner, answered, slipping out of Galactic into the native languageof humans across the twelve home worlds and their colonies. *"Na na, miravela samvar."*

So, we are lost. Navigators skilled enough to independently map solutions when the computers were confused were exceedingly rare, and usually snapped up by the Commonwealth of Stars Battlefleet.

The willow stiffened and lifted her head. She spoke in Galactic. The formality in her tone bespoke something worse. "I beg to report, my lady captain, that a gravitational-spatial disruption is in progress in the sun of this system."

First Mother help us. "Helm, Prepare for jump."

"Destination?" the helmsman intoned, her voice trembling.

"Random sideslip." The reverse of a wormhole scram outside the sidewall of a jump tunnel, and just as dangerous.

"Samson coils spooling up," Tac-0 responded.

"Damage control, prepare for tidal overstress," said the captain. *If only we had a quantum champion on board to shift the probabilities.*

Like a well-tuned machine, the Altari freighter crew, standing tall, gambled with the snapdragon hand fate had dealt them.

The probabilities were not with them and the Altari, who believe in no gods, had none to call on.

The sun brightened athousand-fold, and the expanding corona of a new supernova took the *Castellan* in its embrace and blew her into sparkling motes of flame.

2

THE GIFT

Nations and empires come and go, their life like dust among the stars, but family is forever. -- Constanzia Telluri, mother of Firehill of Altarsha

My father's last gift to me was supposed to help train my visual spatial skills to become a starship pilot. My mother agreed to my practicing with it, but only if I kept my grades up.

The year after my 13th birthday, I sat at a picnic table on the patio of my home, fir trees whispering in the mountain wind above me. I had many math assignments to finish before my homework was done, but I was too excited by my sponsorship to the merchant guild civil space patrol. I would soon fly short missions with my teachers to the inner planets. I hoped to earn a scholarship to the merchant flight school.

I turned my gift, a hand puzzle about the size of kickball, over in my hands. In profile it appeared to have eight sides. My father gave it to me the previous year, before pirates killed him in a raid on his merchant caravan on a run to the outer planets. He had been a minor noble until he married my mother and lost his status. Though he could not command a merchant ship, he had been the best security officer in House Ashastra's merchant fleet.

I twisted and turned the octagonal cubelets round and round under the overcast sky. The pieces gleamed of their own light in shimmering colors as I tried to envision their combinations in my head. Impossible.

My father explained it was a truncated tesseract, a four dimensional representation of an octagon. He told me when my math skills got advanced enough, I could write out the equations, but until then I should practice manually aligning the combinations.

He called it the *omegaoctahedron*, but I called it the O-ball, for short.

I tossed it to the ground and kicked it about. Each time my foot touched it, the surface stabilized, and I dribbled it around the table like a soccer ball.

"Kiryan!" my mother called from the kitchen.

In haste, I stuffed the O-ball into my backpack and opened my data pad to another math problem as she found me.

My mother had an oval face, olive skin and dark brown eyes framed by long black hair that she seldom let down anymore. Ever more worry wrinkles touched her eyes since my father's death.

The frown creases in her forehead smoothed out only when she was hugging me or working theoretical math calculations, or when she sang in that beautiful hypnotic voice that thrummed the chords of my heart every time.

"Did you do your math homework?"

I swallowed, studying the screen hard and mumbling. "Mmmm…"

She inspected my backpack. "Inside," she said.

In the kitchen, I sat as she took the O-ball and set it on the table. The light had gone out of it and it manifested solidity and inertia, just a paperweight the size of a kickball.

"I told you before. Never take that out of the house."

"But why?"

"Isn't it enough that I ask you? Strange things make people talk."

"It's just a stupid toy."

"Don't speak that way about your father's last gift to you."

"Then why can't I take it outside?" I had done it more than once before being caught.

"I want you safe."

I evaded her gaze.

"She took my face in her hands and studied my eyes. "You can't neglect your studies no matter how much you miss him."

I shook my head. "It's impossible. How can you line up eight sides with seven discs?"

"Commoners almost never get into the upper tier schools, child. You have a talent for mathematics, perfect for work as a master navigator."

"I want to pilot ships, not check maps. The computers calculate the jump coordinates."

"Your father accepted his lot and did his duty. When the jump lanes shift and confuse the computers, a mind like yours, if trained to it, can save the ship from being lost. Don't you want to follow his example and help where you are needed most?"

I frowned and shook my head.

"I do not say to ignore your father's gift. The puzzle is more than a training tool. The aliens have kept a secret from humans. Many fear us. The puzzle is a key to why." She laid one hand against the side of my face. I felt the tenderness and the sorrow in her eyes. "But you must not neglect your studies or seek ambitions above your station. I wish your father were here to convince you."

I wanted to find words to comfort her, but none came. "Mother, can we sing a song together now?"

She sniffed and nodded. As her lips parted, she drew in a sharp breath. Her neck jerked, eyes alarmed, her gaze drawn skywards.

My right heel itched like crazy. "What?"

"Come with me now."

She pulled me as the floor shifted. I grabbed the O-ball and backpack as we fled our home. As we crossed the lintel to the outside, the beam cracked in two and fell behind us. A jumbling roar sounded, and the paving stones around the waterfall garden cracked. Fish leaped out of the pond to slap and jump on the ground. A coyote ran downhill yipping in fright.

I took one glance back towards the rumble and the sound of timbers cracking like firecrackers – my house collapsed into rubble. Gone were the Battlefleet pennants on the wall in my bedroom, and the statuettes of famous pilots.

The air shrieked with a rising wind, and we staggered. A cliff of rock above our home studded with Joshua trees cracked, gaps opening in it that swallowed the ancient trees that had survived thunderstorm, hail, blizzards, but not this.

Below us, a fissure opened in the pavement that widened and snaked down the street, parting it. People screamed and scattered, caught between falling buildings and the widening earth that swallowed them up. An old woman pushed a handcart, swaying on her feet as the street shook. A mother clutching her infant to her breast ran up to us, wild eyed, eyes darting and reached a hand out. She screamed as the pavement fractured and half the street fell away into a pit, taking her with it. Aghast, I stumbled as my mother pulled me back and dragged me with her. We ran.

Concrete power poles shivered like jello, wires snapping and sparking as the lines contorted like writhing snakes, electrocuting the hapless caught in their fall.

We were caught between heaven and earth with nowhere to go. Mother's eyes searched, intent and she held out an arm, singing low. For the briefest seconds, a sinuous pattern glittered on her right arm, one I had seen a few times while working the puzzle of the O-ball.

"This way." She pulled me without mercy, navigating the falling stone and twisting cables, the shifting cracks, with the foresight she tapped from the ancient songs. Men and women clutched at us as we passed like ghosts through hell. An avalanche of rock rolled down towards us from my buried house.

I thought we would make it down to lower ground, to plazas wide enough to avoid the falling buildings collapsing.

Mother pulled up short and gasped.

A hundred feet away, a woman stood. She wore a light armor combat suit, like I had seen in space marine recruiting posters, like the ones on posters in my bedroom. She was young, not much older than me, with long blond hair. The body suit had no marking or colors I recognized, black and tan. She ignored the mayhem as if she stood at the center of the eye of a hurricane and we with her. Something seemed wrong with the air around her, a shimmering of light barely visible. She pointed a gauntleted finger at us. My backpack pulled away, the straps pulling me around and dragging me behind it towards the strange woman. Fires erupted from broken gas lines, geysers of flame rising around us.

I dug my heels in; straining towards my mother who reached for me with her left hand. My heel burned as she stretched out her right arm and hummed, subvocalizing words in ancient Altari unfamiliar to me. The pressure eased and I took a step towards her.

I looked over my shoulder at the other woman.

She drew a pistol and fired. The plasma bolt sheared past my ear crackling like lightning. I flinched. My mother gasped. The force on my pack redoubled its pull on me and only my mother's hysterical strength held me in place.

A fierce anger ignited in her eyes, and she sang. A twilight dark fell around us as if we stood in a circle of dusk. She sang aloud now her right hand stretched towards the enemy who was lining up another shot with her pistol. For a moment the tattoo of a feathered serpent flickered like lightning on the inside of my mother's right forearm. My right heel burned like molten lava, and I bit my lip in pain.

My mother sang and a sheet of flame rose between us and the stranger. The force on me disappeared. Mother pulled me into a building that leaned at a crazy angle, shale tiles falling and breaking all around us.

"No." I said, balking.

"Inside now."

"We'll be buried."

"The only way out...Trust me!"

I hesitated, frightened. She dragged me by main force, as panicking I resisted, slowing us down. A cracking sound ripped above. Dust drifted down from the ceiling. She tried to pull my hand. I froze.

The crack widened and dust poured down on us. A horrible rumbling sound shook the air. Plaster fell in sheets.

"Kiryan!" she cried out as the ceiling caved in.

I awoke, blood trickling into my face from a gash on my head. A beam lay across my chest pinning me. My mother groaned. She stood up from the floor, eyes searching.

"Mother." I forced the word out with the last of my breath.

She clawed her way to me. The side of her head was bloody, her beautiful black hair matted with it. She heaved at the beam, too heavy to budge.

She commanded. "Push with me. Lift."

I tried. The beam was crushing the air out of me.

She staggered to her feet trying with all her might to lift the beam without effect. The blood had soaked the side of her head and trickled down her neck. Her skin turned pale, a deathly white. She fell to her knees.

I was afraid for myself and ashamed. She was hurt, and I couldn't help her. My chest caved in from the crushing weight. I gasped but no air came. My lungs burned, and my heart pounded like thunder. Cold sweat drenched my clothes and my vision grayed at the edges, as my forehead bled.

My mother yanked the shoe off my right foot and ripped off the sock. She slumped forward, and with an outstretched hand her palm pressed against my right heel, the one with the dragon tattoo.

"Sing," she whispered. She sang, a melody she had taught me.

I mouthed her words, barely able to echo them with my last breath, so dizzy, almost gone. My heel grew warm, then my whole body shivered, and images cascaded into my mind, thousands upon thousands of images of every conceivable place, strobing into me too fast to count. Stars and suns, trees, rain, storms, ghettos and sea docks, myriad peoples, and aliens as if suddenly I beheld every place everywhere at once. I was able to take a breath. My voice strengthened and I joined in her song.

More images raced through my mind, too many, too fast to understand. Runes of an ancient language whirling about in a lightning storm, rain falling, falling, falling, drowning the world. A roar of flame and flashing teeth and serpent eyes. Glowing white, fogs and mists choking slopes of ash, and the rising of a white-hot sun too bright to endure.

A pitiless guilt rose like a tidal wave for a nameless sin damning me forever.

"Push" she whispered.

The beam eased away in a single thrust of my arms.

"Mother, you did it." She lay prone, unmoving. Shadows crossed the room as dusk fell over the ruined town.

The power was out. Outside wailed the screams of the dying, and moans of despair. Night fell, and in the mountains, things crept and stalked, and they were hungry.

In the flickering light of the fires, I turned my mother over, and her eyes stared lifeless. I fell across her body and wept, long shuddering groans, until I passed out.

3

Awakening

A lovely song in a grace-filled woman's voice thrummed my heart. Distant, so distant, a trumpet called from the center of a burning light that exploded. I stirred. I blinked half-open eyes with lashes clotted by stinging yellow scales. A pink-blue glow of indirect lights around the ceiling waxed out, replaced by a white light bright in its bleakness. I lay in a strange bed. How long had I been here?

My bare arms and legs trembled, almost disconnected from me. I was naked under a thin cotton gown and sick to my stomach.

I tried to remember what had happened to me. A roaring sound. Falling and crushing sensations. Horror. Grief. Nurses in white shoes and stern faces had come and gone during the days that followed. At night, robot med techs patrolled, the whirling sounds of metal wheels waking me out of a dreadful sleep. A black boot, hard as a seashell, wrapped my right leg from the knee down. Looped straps held the front and back pieces together.

Mom? Where was my mother? I had to find her. She would know my name.

I sat up in bed, elated at my success. My head spun, but the dizziness settled quickly. Holding to my resolve, I ignored the headache that rose like a wave trying to press me back down. My vision was clearing. Fear started a fire in my chest. I turned it to anger against a faceless enemy.

I recognized the door only when it slid open with a hissing sound. An enormous man, dressed in white tunic and trousers, with meaty hands and a scarred face, walked in. He looked surprised. "You're awake."

I sniffed. "I guess I am."

"Damn night shift."

"Where am I?"

"Stay put. I'll find a nurse." He left the room. The door slid shut.

Will you? Where is my mother? A glowing octagonal shape rose in my mind's eye.

I eased out of the bed. My legs firmer now. I unstrapped the boot, and it fell apart into two pieces, which I threw aside. I tested my legs, stiff as gears stuck in glue. I worked them, flexing and extending my knees, and they trembled and jerked with the effort. The stiffness eased, but my right heel itched like hell. I sat and grabbed my foot to scratch it and froze at the sight of the tatoo.

My bisnonn, my great-grandmother, had tattooed my heel on my fourth birthday even as my parents pleaded with her to wait. A dragon flying over the sea towards a five petaled lily in the sky. I remembered the burning pain, the struggle, my outraged cries. Bisnonn's eyes glistening with unshed tears, her jaw set. "Bear it child, lest the universe end before its time."

The door opened. A nurse, this one in a noble house uniform, with an orange and black sash. A military nurse. My home world's flag was green and white. She carried a tray with an injection syringe. "Sit down. It's time for your medication."

I stalled. My head was clearing. "Aren't you supposed to make sure I'm the right patient, like ask my name before you give me that?"

The orderly had followed her in. He seized my left wrist and held it up. I was wearing a plastic ID wristband with no name, only a code pattern. She smiled and scanned it with a handheld device. It blinked green. "You're the right boy."

Lucky me. "No. Don't touch me."

"Lie down. You've been injured."

"Not before you bring my mother."

The nurse shook her head. "She can't come."

"Why not? Who put me here?" My voice rose in pitch and cracked on the last word.

"Don't make this difficult."

She had the exasperated look of a schoolteacher talking down to a slow learner. I needed time. I tried to bargain. "Why do I need that? Don't you want to know what I remember about the accident?" *Not much. Maybe she can tell me.*

"A doctor can ask you later. Sit down."

"How about asking me now? You don't need to give me a shot. I feel fine." *I can't take much more of this.*

"Will you just be quiet and do as I say?"

"I'm not letting you do anything to me without mother's permission."

She looked at the orderly and jerked her chin towards me. A signal. He reached for me. I yelled.

He grabbed my shoulders. "Hold still, you peon."

He tried to pin my arms back. I flailed. He was too strong for me to fight fair. My knee came up hard, driving it into his nether parts. He groaned, and he flinched enough for me to roll off the bed.

I ran for the door and came up short. Locked. I turned; the nurse was speaking in a low voice to her collar tab. The orderly's face looked mad enough to hurt me.

My mother had taught me songs. My father had taught me to fight. I remembered the drills, over and over since I could walk. Though I had forgotten my name, my muscles remembered the forms. Shouting something in the old tongue, I charged him and attacked, striking fast as a thunderbolt and twice as hard.

The orderly lay moaning on the floor, cradling his left forearm with his right, the arm bent fork-shaped at an angle. The nurse cowered on the floor in a corner. "What kind of boy are you?"

I approached her, breathing hard, fists clenched. "Tell me my name if you don't want to learn more." Was she an enemy or just doing her job? Any second others might come through the door. I went down on one knee, bent my face closer to hers. "Get my mother now."

She jabbed my left shoulder with the needle. I batted it away. My right hand gripped her throat, squeezing. Her eyes bulged, and she gagged. Shocked by my rage, I released her. She sputtered. "Kiryan. Your name is Kiryan Telluri." The name, familiar yet strange, left me doubting.

"Bring me to my mother."

The nurse shook her head.

"Tell me." My face heated, I ground my teeth in a grimace.

"You can't go to her. She died saving you."

I remembered. Vertigo seized me. I slumped over and I resisted not at all as two more orderlies and a med tech dressed me. They strapped me into a mechanized wheelchair and took me away.

4

TRAPPED

I tried to keep my eyes open. The hallway was white walled with sliding auto doors like the room they took me out of. The wheelchair drove itself, following a young, ghostlike woman holding a signet wand whose steady green light hurt my eyes to look at. I fought the drug from the shot and bit my lower lip for the pain to wake me. The man whose arm I had just broken turned left down a corridor. We kept going.

The nurse's shoes made a crisp snicking sound like a sarpanya rock drake picking its teeth. Drakes lurked in the uplands above my home. Up north, that was where I was from.

To my left, a man in gray fatigues strode, a pistol on his right hip. I did not know enough to tell what kind of gun. We passed two more doors on the left and one on the right. At the end of the hall, steel double doors parted, and we entered another white walled room.

A woman, a noble dressed in black surcoat and pleated skirt, sat behind an oaken desk whose pedestals were carved with intertwined vines, trees, horses galloping in a hunt, comets, and starships. A comm link on her flaring collar. An orange and gold stola draped over her shoulders with lettering marking exploits and achievements.

My mind swam in circles, trying to remember if those were colors of a Great House or not. *Kiryan Telluri, I am, I am.* My head buzzed. The nurse left.

Across from the noble sat a tall man sat with his back to me. Dressed in a buff-colored suit, simple, tailored nice like a well-to-do commoner would wear. He leaned towards the noble, finishing a sentence as I entered. "I've done my part, now do yours." He stiffened, turned as my chair came alongside him. "Hello, nephew."

That voice, that face belonged to my father's brother. My tongue stuck to the roof of my mouth, a cotton sensation gagging me.

He frowned. "My Lady, what have you done to him?"

She was Great House nobility.

Her voice was gritty yet velvety. "Conditions have changed. We must take the boy."

My head was clearing. I last saw my uncle the day after my tattooing. He and my father had been shouting at each other in an argument outside my room that drifted away with their footsteps. He had called my father a fool.

"What conditions?"

"He broke the orderly's arm like a branch and almost throttled his nurse."

"Look at him. How could he?"

"We heard the words through the comm link. He spoke words in ancient Altari. Who taught him? Be content that I do not bring you under interdiction."

My uncle sagged in his chair. He pursed his lips and rubbed his forehead, brushing salt and pepper hair back. "Very well, but I'll claim my right to say goodbye to him."

She nodded.

"Alone."

"I will give you a privacy screen. Five minutes while we watch. "

My uncle nodded like a defeated gladiator kneeling before his executioner. The noblewoman motioned to the signet wand holder, who pressed a device on her belt. A screen wafted up, looking like wrinkled air. The room beyond it looked like stalking shadows.

"Nephew."

"You left us alone when she needed family."

He sighed and shook his head.

"Now my mother is dead." My sorrow was stronger than any tonic. I would have stood up and attacked him, but they had manacled my wrists to the chair's arms.

"You are passionate, like your father. Now listen to me if you want to live."

I frowned, a frightening rage simmering in my breast. My right heel warmed, the rest of me icy cold.

"I hope they are too proud to breach a privacy screen, so listen. After the earthquake, they found your mother beside you. She was dead of a head injury, but she must have signaled for help first, and saved you, because a light drew the rescue brigade to your home."

My eyes stung and blinked like shutters on a zoetrope.

"Your body was not with her, and I feared the worst. I searched for you for weeks. Finally, that woman sent her lackey, the one with the wand, claiming to be from a medical transport team, and brought you here."

"And you believed her?"

"Stop judging. Your rashness risks death. I met with her boss, and she demanded information from me. I tried to save you."

Confusion mixed with a turmoil of shattered memory. "She said she is taking me."

"Great House nobility has no shame in lying to common folk like us. It might have gone otherwise if you hadn't gone antimatter on them."

"Who? Why?"

"They may be impersonating another house. Maybe, they're pirates."

He bent low, hands on my shoulders, and whispered. "Can you run?"

I flexed my calf muscles. "Hmmm." I looked at the manacles.

Keeping his body between the chair and the watchers outside the screen, my uncle touched a black box over a square of metal on the side of the wheelchair. The manacles clicked and their pressure relaxed from my wrists.

"Follow my lead and if our escape separates us, run to the capital, to the merchant guild house. Tell no one your real name. I will find you later."

"Mother said that if I learned my math and mastered the O-ball that I could make a difference someday to help keep the peace."

"You can't become a starship pilot, forget that."

"I was supposed to start lessons next week with the civil space patrol. If I don't show, no one will ever accept me for training ever again."

"My fool brother and his ideas. I'm sorry, nephew. The region is a disaster zone. No one will be giving you lessons."

"My father said I could be a great navigator."

"You can't be safe if you do that. Forget your dreams."

"No."

"From now on, your last name is Toragni. I'll help you build a life as a merchant under their radar."

Voice cracking. "Toragni? Toragni."

"In Galactic it means Firehill. Our codeword. A finger to the eye of our enemy."

Uncle clasped my head in both hands and pressed his forehead to mine. "I'm sorry I abandoned my brother. I will make up for it if I can. Once we break out, if you should find yourself alone, go to Urbmar and find a merchant to apprentice with. You will be safe until I come to you."

The field sparkled.

My uncle stood as the field dissipated. I sagged, head down, wrists still in their place. My new name echoed in my mind like a song by my mother, Toragni, Firehill in Galactic. I raised my head and looked the noble in the eye. I held her glance for seconds, trying to see into her black heart. She stared back, face calm. I did not look away. She broke from my glance and looked at the man with the pistol. "Take him."

Uncle stood and bowed. "Forgive me if I leave now noble lady."

His tone was insolent. The ghostlike woman frowned. The man in the gray fatigues put a hand on my uncle's shoulder. "Is that a way to talk to the First Sister?"

"Silence." The noblewoman hissed the word out. He might have said what world she was from with that title. Uncle erupted into action.

Uncle elbowed the armsman in the throat and executed the Monsoon Snake form with alacrity and perfection, spinning behind him as the blonde woman's dagger plunged into the armsman's chest. He ripped the dead man's pistol from his holster and fired back. The blonde ducked and rolled, and his laser pulses pocked the wall.

Her swiftness was breathtaking, and as she dodged, she drew a long knife from a concealed scabbard. Flame rippled along one edge, and a lacelike web of light shimmered on her knife arm as the techno blade synchronized to her. To even touch such a weapon would earn me a death sentence.

My uncle snatched the signet wand up from the floor and pivoted. He pushed it into my hands as I stood free of the chair. "Run!

I ran, wand held up to key the doorway. Uncle followed, blasting cover fire as we fled the room.

5

ESCAPE

I held up the wand the way I had seen the blonde woman using it. My uncle shouted instructions. "All the way to the corridor branch, then run to the end of the hall." I fought the urge to look back, my mouth dry, my heart racing. We ran up to the first door on my right. The signet light went from red to green. What if? I scuffed my heels, stopping, almost losing my footing. My uncle nearly collided with me.

"I said down the hall!"

I faced the door, and it slid open. A storeroom with empty boxes.

"Didn't you hear me? Run." My uncle shoved me back on course. He turned and fired a salvo of laser bolts. The door we had come through still shut.

I hurried to the next door. The earthquake was an accident, but they wanted me because of what they found, so they must have taken it.

"By the mothers, what are you doing?"

"They took something from me. Maybe it's in one of these rooms."

"Wherever they took it, forget it. We have to reach the shuttle bay."

Shuttle? Are we in orbit? I stared at the next door. "I have to find it." Even as I checked the third door in the hall, they had taken me down and found it full of medical supplies. Laser fire sizzled behind me. I turned. My uncle was shooting at the blond woman. As the laser flashed, her flaming knife absorbed the beams that hissed as they struck, bending the path of the light to miss her.

My uncle grabbed the signet wand from me and, panting, said. "She's a noble house assassin. She is wielding a Deekathi spire dagger, and I can't beat that. Come with me." He pushed me forward.

We ran together and then rounded the corner, legs pumping, chests heaving, trying to make distance. Another door on our left opened, and the orderly walked out wearing a splint and sling. He looked surprised, maybe afraid, and retreated into the room. The nurse was behind him. My fear drove me, and I ran faster, my uncle trying to keep up.

At the end of a long corridor, at least ten meters, we came to a circular steel hatch. It dilated open. We ran into an open space, like a warehouse framed with girders and dotted with pallets of gear covered under red tarps. Tool carts. A med tech robot unloading the pallets, ignoring us. My uncle used a wrench to break a plate on the wall next to the hatch. It winked shut. A ringing sounded in the chamber. "That may hold them long enough."

He led me double time to a hatch big enough to drive three air cars through. He punched a protruding button the size of my hand and the hatch opened. I spied another door to our left.

The enemy might catch us. I should have listened to my uncle. But I had to *know*. As his task distracted him, I picked the signet wand off the deck and ran to the door. Uncle cursed behind me as the door slid open. The object of my desire floated above a metal cube, a glittering, shimmering object about the size of a child's kickball, many colored octagonal 'cubelets' made up the surface.

My uncle caught up with me. "What the hell is that?"

I reached for it.

"Stop, it has a security field. Let's go."

"Not without it."

"We don't have time."

"I need it."

"More than living?"

"That's all I have left of them."

Muttering profanities under his breath, my uncle applied the device he used to free me to the side of the marble box. Numbers scrolled. He unfolded a programming pad. More numbers scrolled. The ball fell to the surface, active again, the cubelets moving in crisscrossing axial lines, drifting. I picked it up. As soon as I touched it, it stabilized into a solid object again.

My dad called it the omegaoctahedron. A slap to the side of my head stung.

"Fool boy, let's go."

We left the room. The hatch had opened to a hangar bay with windows letting in the harsh white light like Altarsha's sun. Two surface to space shuttles sat on landing skids. One of them had mercantile guild markings. My uncle pointed to it. He was about to say something, then he grimaced and shuddered. The blonde assassin had caught up with us. She stabbed my uncle in the back again with that flaming knife. Flesh burned and clothing charred as she pulled it out. The wounds did not bleed.

My uncle was still standing but had turned white. He tried to elbow his attacker, but she twisted free and he toppled to the floor and lay still. She bent over him as she looked me in the eye with a thin smile on her face and drew back to stab him again.

No. No. NO. Not again. Please, mother of mothers.

Her eyes shifted to the ball in my hand, with sudden interest. She pushed my uncle aside and sheathed the knife. Lunged for me with both hands. No ideas came to me as I backpedaled. I agonized about what to do. I held it up. "If you want this so bad, lady, take it."I threw the omegaoctahedron far across the bay — toward the shuttles, making up a plan as I went. She ground her teeth and ran for the device. I went to my uncle. "Get up, uncle, please." He didn't move. I went to Plan B.

As the assassin went for my gift, I ran towards the shuttle. I scrambled past her and kicked the ball into the open hatch. It bounced and almost missed, but I scored a goal and the last bounce took it into the shuttle. I sealed the hatch. I knew how my father had thought about these things. He had been a security officer. I sat in the pilot's chair and slammed a palm down on the pilot control board. The ship was in a hot unload status. The control board lit up. Well, I always wanted to be a starship pilot.

I cracked my knuckles and took hold of the helm.

The shuttle hovered, nose yawing slightly. A tactical display shimmered in a heads up display in the lower half of the canopy, and through the transparent glass my uncle's body in view, but not the assassin. I scanned the HUD's readings to find three life sign readings in the hangar. My uncle was still alive. But where was the assassin, and who was the third person? Duh. I guess me, if I live through this.

A thump on the hull. Another thump. The assassin?

The shuttle attitude control made sense, a dial that turned on a base that canted in two dimensions. I turned the dial a few degrees, and the shuttle spun slowly. Another thump.

I wondered what noble house assassins could do? Maybe she was a mercenary, a hireling from one of the outer planet pirate groups that made a living raiding merchants and taking hostages. I jerked the dial in a longer twist and the shuttle spun 360 degrees, almost flipping. An indicator light flashed red. Mothers, I have no clue what I'm doing.

Ideas swarmed in my mind like a cloud of hornets. Should I press a panic button and hope the shuttle would autopilot to a safe zone? *No!*

My uncle needed help. Was he even still alive? Where would I take him? I wasn't even sure I was on my home world.

Mother, what do I do? I cut the power, and the shuttle lurched down. I hoped for a lucky break. Maybe the shuttle would squash my attacker under a skid. Little chance of that. My uncle was leaning on one elbow, shaking his head.

I remembered a melody my mother had taught me and hummed it to myself, from a ballad about some ancient hero of forgotten name. Plan C didn't leave me very hopeful. Fight or die.

I rummaged through a tool locker, precious seconds gone. I put on a safety vest, stuffed its pockets, cycled the hatch and jumped out fast as a scared cat, and ran towards my uncle, looking about me for the enemy. I spotted her at the other shuttle, about to enter it. Our eyes met. She left the shuttle to rush me. I ran to my uncle's side

He groaned. "Damn fool boy, save yourself."

The rebuke in his voice was so like my father's. My hands shook. Still, I thought this might be a good time to start listening to his advice. "Sure, uncle, both of us." We hobbled for our shuttle. No way we would beat the assassin to our ship. I guess she did not think me much of a threat. She had not even bothered to draw a weapon. Faster that way.

Dismissed by another adult. No threat at all. But my father made me learn how to be a threat even when I didn't feel like it. And now, I felt like it.

"Sorry, uncle." I pulled the laser blaster secured under his belt and fired a volley of bolts at the assassin. She deserved it.

She ducked and rolled and even somersaulted once. It was a beautiful thing to watch. At least I had slowed her down. I clambered up the shuttle ladder and, using a rope from my vest under my uncle's arms, I helped him climb the rest of the way. He was still pale white, covered in sweat, and staggered into the pilot's seat.

I wondered what this was all about. Too many memories stirred up. My parents pushing me but never saying why — always urgent, scared like something terrible would happen. And the years before bisnonn died, up to when I was eight years old, looking at me so often frowning and shaking her head. I baited her. Why? Why? Why, bisnonn? She would raise her hand to slap me, but I was too fast and dodged. If I dodged fast enough, she might smile and say maybe the universe wouldn't end before its time. Disappointing her left a bitter memory that tasted like gall. Why had she laid that burden on me?

I tucked the omegaoctohedron away inside the tool locker. I swayed as the shuttle lifted and I tumbled into the copilot's chair and strapped in.

Uncle squeezed my shoulder. "Hang on." He entered numbers on a pad. Grimaced. "We're lucky this is a civilian hangar."

"Where are we?" The shuttle started a slow acceleration towards the closed hangar doors. They started to open.

"Altarsha. Not that far from where your house was."

"It creeps me out how that lady never said a word."

"My guess is she has a neural implant and her mind was occupied, being a channel for her boss."

"That's worse."

He pushed a throttle and the acceleration force pushed me back into my seat as we catapulted out of the bay into a clear blue sky lit by harsh white sunlight, over pine forested rocky slopes.

The comm monitor came alive with broken voice cadences, mathematical sequences switching rapidly. A series of squeals and burps.

"Uncle?"

"Encrypted military communications." He throttled the engines to full power.

6

PURSUIT

The familiar terrain reminded me of home. It was home. Pieces of memory floated like shining fragments of broken glass, too sharp to touch. I hurt bad, grieving. How could I keep up the courage my uncle thought so much of?

He handled the shuttle with ease, but he looked like he wouldn't last. "Uncle, where do we go now?"

He gritted out the words, one by one, punctuated by gasps. "Up... higher, into the transport grid sensors."

I had read lots of comics about pirates and the galactic Battlefleet. "Shouldn't we send a distress call?"

"Not yet. The other shuttle launched and I don't want to draw them in easier than I need to."

A *deetle deetle* sound rang out from the console. A soft feminine voice from the shuttle computer said ever so calmly. "Radar lock. Radar lock."

"Shit!" My uncle rammed the helm pedestal forward and dove the shuttle. Snowcapped peaks loomed as we dove. A vapor trail passed on my right and the shuttle bucked.

The control board was not very complicated on a shuttle. I examined the switches and indicator text. I should help, but how?

Another sound, a warble like a strangling swallow. A green light flashed. "Should we answer that?"

"Buy us time, Kiryan, bullshit them." He barrel rolled and twisted the shuttle up towards the sun. My head ached, and the maneuver left me nauseated. I toggled the communicator. A hologram materialized in front of my seat. It was the noble that had imprisoned me. She wore a black and silver flight suit without insignia. Golden light gleamed in tendrils along her shoulders and other parts of the suit. A gorge of fear rose in my throat.

The image looked at me. Her field of view covered me and my immediate location, but not my uncle. "Mr. Joort, hand over the prisoner and his toy." It irritated me to be ignored. "Hey, noble lady, I'm not going with you."

The noble nodded. "I don't mind killing you, stripling, but I don't want to damage your cargo."

"Uncle, she's wearing a Battlefleet flight suit."

"Just hope she doesn't have any house guard military with her. Almost there."

I tried to distract her. "That ball belongs to me and only I know how to use it."

"Perhaps. Perhaps not."

I thought the omegaoctahedron was just a three-dimensional math puzzle to train my mind. Yet neither of my parents ever said that. I just assumed it was because I kept pestering them about wanting to be a starship pilot when I grew up. Oh well, he said to bullshit her. "Yah, right First Sister. What if I already solved it?"

Her eyes widened. Not afraid, but wary. "Last chance. The device has survived countless years. I doubt your wreckage will hurt it."

"Almost there." My uncle toggled the distress beacon.

The computer warned. "Radar lock. Radar lock."

"Almost." The shuttle altitude indicator gained another hundred meters.

"Collision imminent."

We barrel rolled again. A roaring sound. The shuttle heaved, stalled, and dropped its nose. I lifted in my straps, held down against the negative g forces. My uncle slumped in his seat, unresponsive. I fought the ship, jerking back on the helm wheel, pulling the yoke back towards my body. The nose came up, and we drifted up. I over corrected, and the nose fell again as I activated the emergency landing autopilot.

Flexible airfoils inflated on either side of the shuttle with a palpable thump. The tensile fabric rippled as the computer worked the ailerons to make a survivable landing. Red telltale indicators flashed across the board.

If I was going to die, I did not want her to have the satisfaction of picking over my bones. Of course, my chances of survival went down by at least half if I tried it. What would my chances be if I were still alive only to be found by her? That settled the decision for me. I hummed a tune and flipped up a targeting monocle. I used a joystick to paint a landing zone, a narrow crevasse in a steep rock face.

I sang well as a child, but my voice had changed as I grew last year, and I couldn't sing now worth beans. Screw it. Grieving for my mother. I sang a dirge about a hero who lost his true love to death. I sounded awful, even to myself, but it steadied me.

Almost to the crevasse. An airfoil broke loose, setting the shuttle into a tumble. We didn't break up on the first impact. As the world turned like a mad gyroscope, we plunged down the cracked rock into the dark.

We bounced down a shaft; the hull striking walls of stone with grinding and buckling groans. G-forces tugged six ways in my five point straps and nausea grabbed my throat and shook my insides as well. The shaft wasn't vertical and the slope, though steep, allowed us to tumble and break our fall enough that when we finally came to rest at a thirty degree tilt, I was still conscious. I smelled burnt insulation. The emergency lights were on, glowing amber-red inside. Outside the windows, the square of light only showed scattered boulders a few feet away, the rest graying out into a pit of darkness.

The tool locker's door lay ajar, twisted, and the omegaoctahedron lay on the deck, shining and glittering, the glowing colored octagonal cubelets moving in linear crisscrossing circles, the colors mixing and remixing. On each side twinkled a single gem that meandered with the cubelets. However the shapes recombined, there was only one gem per side, seven gems in total wandering over the eight sides. It hearkened mystery to me, questions my parents had not lived long enough to answer.

I turned to my uncle and unbuckled the straps holding him. The action roused him and he gasped and opened his eyes. He coughed, to his skin's pallor now added blue lips. He motioned with one hand, thumb and little finger extended, touching his thumb to his parched mouth.

"A drink? You want a drink?" I rummaged through a survival pack, standard issue, and broke open a flask seal and held it to his lips. The attempt to drink the water set him coughing again. He pushed the flask away. The spout had flecks of blood on it.

"Nephew..."

"Yes, uncle?"

"You bullshit pretty good." He groaned. "I launched a distress drone and a tight beam through the grid relay to the paraman's base star. Maybe a constable dispatcher will pick it one or the other on the grid and fish you out of this pit."

I shivered, my heart pounded. "Both of us, right, sir?"

He shook his head. "If they don't, or if yonder enemy comes down after you, take as much as food and water as you can carry and find a way out underground."

"I don't understand."

"You dropped us into an air shaft for an old mine. Shafts, pits, and caverns riddle the Shield Mountains. f you hear water, follow it."

"What if I don't?"

"Then find another way."

"How?"

"That's not my problem anymore." His eyes shone, reflecting the light from the omegaoctahedron. "Whatever that thing is, a Great House has trespassed against our world to chase it down. They would risk vendetta or worse and sent a First Sister to get it. Do you know what that means?"

First Sisters were second in command of their homeworld's government, one of the twenty-four most powerful women in human space. "No uncle."

"There's no one left to help you fight this kind of enemy. You are a minnow flung into a pool of sharks. Make yourself as small as possible and disappear."

"What about our plan?" I was desperate not to accept what was happening.

"Remember your family, but forget your name. You are Kiryan Toragni, Firehill from now on. Go to Urbmar and apprentice to a trustworthy merchant." He laughed, coughed. "There are some honest ones."

"Who will teach me if you leave me?"

"There are guild houses and diplomats at the capital. You will find aliens there. If you can't find an honest merchant, go find a harirossa to apprentice you. The buggers can't stop singing and writing poetry. Be wary of whom you trust. And let no one see that tattoo on your heel, unless you already know you can trust your life with them."

Who? How? There is so much I don't know. I would have asked another question, but he was gone.

7

HUNTED

G rief, uncalled for, unwanted, irresistible, churned inside me. Darkness fell across my eyes and my head hung, mouth open, breathing hard. I knelt beside my uncle and took one of his hands in mine and lifted it to press against my forehead. I held it there in silence. How long I don't know. I came out of my stupor when light flared in my peripheral vision. I looked up. The omegaoctahedron shone with many-colored beams that dotted the shuttle cabin with points of light, like constellations in the night sky. White light burned at the borders of the cubelets, too bright to stare at directly.

What had come over it? I touched one hand to the now solid surface, and an invisible spark touched my fingers. The ball returned to its shifting forms, and I pondered the choices before me.

The republic considered me a man, subject to vendetta, and my enemy would rather kill me if she couldn't use me. After how they had drugged me in the hospital, what might they do if they took me alive? Uncle, why did you have to die? Did I kill you with my stubbornness? I knew I had. Guilt clawed at me. And if I had run sooner, he might have died anyway and lost the last tie to my parents.

A shower of dust fell through the shaft of light to the side of the crashed shuttle. Then flickering of light and dark. Someone would come down after me, if only to make sure I was dead and retrieve the o-ball. But my uncle had sent out a distress call. Someone would investigate, but would it be in time? And how would I know to trust them? I agonized.

If I stayed put, I might await rescue or ensure my capture. If I left, where would I go?

The shuttle, silent as a mausoleum, weighed on me. I heard running water.

I shrugged my shoulders. My uncle wanted me to try, so I would. Besides, I was thirsty.

I used to think my parents were hard on me. Mother made me study mathematics until I solved Fourier transforms in my head. Father taught me other forms in martial arts — the stalking crane, the howling monkey, the night banshee. I never knew why they were so driven or why bisnonn seemed scared, the universe would end. Why? So pushed, I never did good enough to satisfy my parents. For a while, I wondered if they loved me.

Something inside me snarled. One time, my mother almost threw out my Battlefleet flag collection. Told me there were better things to do with my life than chasing pirates or subjugating rebellious planets. But Battlefleet keeps the peace, I told her, and I can be a starship pilot. Only nobles can join Battlefleet, she said. She was going to tell me more, then looked sad and never finished the sentence. No chance remained now to ask her or to finish untaught lessons. I might have asked uncle, but now he was gone.

My heel burned. The dragon tattoo. Why? Who am I? I said to the shadows. Something cold entered my heart. Resolving the impossible, I vowed I would find a way to Mahara and learn everything the galactic academy could teach me. Earning a place in the Jaguar Bow Sword as a Battlefleet pilot would give me status and power beyond the limits of my family and station. One day I would find out who that woman was who just killed the last of my family, and bring her and her conspirators to justice.

I stuffed the o-ball into a backpack and filled the remaining space with food ration packs. There were no weapons, so I made do with emergency flares and a pry bar. A torch with fresh batteries would have to suffice for light. I might be a man, but by the mothers, I needed a few more years to grow big enough to fight these kinds of enemies.***

I hummed a tune my mother taught me. It reverberated into the air, magnified I suppose by the cavern. Heat rose in my chest and the weight of the surrounding rock pressed down on my bones.

For a moment, I felt like a giant. The moment passed, and I set off with a torchlight into the dark towards the water.

A mechanical sound like hiccups followed by pinging sounds sounded from up the shaft we had fallen down. Crystals on the walls fluoresced as a metallic ball fell onto the shuttle, sticking to its roof. The pinging stopped and the profile of the sphere pulsed red at a slowly increasing frequency.

I stumbled, following the sound of the running water running only a few feet. I pulled out the electric torch and focused the beam. Rocky dirt sloped downwards, opening into a cavern with a roof receding into shadow as I clambered down.

A sudden heaviness to the backpack dragged like a leaden weight and pulled me down hard, knocking the wind out of me. I tasted pebbles and grit. Air boomed and heat washed over my back scorching the hairs on my neck. The cavern ahead lit in orange as flames dissipated in fiery streams, revealing the openings of two tunnels.

The tunnel on my left had a gentle upward slope, the other on the right dropped in broken shale, the water following its slope in rivulets and little cascades and swirling pools. Pinging behind me. Another of those balls rolled into the space, pulsing red.

My back pack lighter now, the torch squeezed tight in my fingers; I rose and shifted from side to side. The closeness to the surface tempted me to move to higher ground. Up was safer I thought. The ball pulsed red, faster and faster.

Fire was coming. As the clicking increased in frequency I flung myself down the slope towards the water. A boom shook the tunnel and red heat bloomed at my back. A titan's slap stunned me and lifted my body into the air.

I coughed, sputtering and choking from the pool of water in which I lay on my side. Thanking the first mothers that it was too shallow to drown in, I sat up and raked my hand through my hair. The torch glowed under the surface and I retrieved it. Exploring the broken shale revealed the chamber had three other tunnels besides the one I had come down. Something crunched under my feet, white and splintered, a bone with bits of flesh hanging off. I threw it away.

A click-clack sound came the way I had fallen. This orb walked on spider mechanical legs and the red circle light strobed left and right.

I sneezed.

The light fixed in my direction, and a barely audible hum issued from the orb. I dashed for a tunnel, which one I didn't care. A plasma bolt shattered the spot where I had been kicking up more bones and water spurts. I rolled towards another tunnel. A bolt struck it and rocks collapsed, blocking the way.

I crab walked backwards, hyperventilating. No. No.

The spider thing skittered closer to me, the red eye scanning me. My right heel burned like fire, too painful to bear. I put it into the water. The light fixed on me and the hum started.

Heart leaped in my chest, bounding like a fleeing gazelle. A scalloped shadow spread behind the search and destroy bomb. Luminous red slanted lights appeared and steam rose, hissing. I flinched. A whoosh sounded, then a stream of red-white fire lashed at the bomb and melted it into a metal pool.

The new intruder, serpentine with great clawed haunches and shimmering red scales, shuffled forward and sniffed at me. I had trespassed into a sarpanya's lair.

8

— · —

SARPANYA

Sarpanyas are the smaller cousins of the great dragons that used to be seen on Altarsha an age ago, rock drakes to alien visitors. Out worlders prize them for exhibit in galactic menageries. The last party to capture one was a company of alien soldiers — sarpan hunters armed with energy weapons and battle armor, two centuries earlier. Out of the hundred that entered the mines, only two survived, and one of them died later from her burns. No one had ever caught a sarpanya since, nor ever tamed one. I feared it was hungry for dinner with no viable alternative but me in the vicinity.

It waddled over to me and nosed my backpack and looked up at me with liquid yellow eyes and slitted pupils. I flipped open the rucksack and spread the field rations out in a fan before it. It snuffled at it with flaring nostrils braced by feelers like a catfish.

"What? That's the best I can do."

It rumbled its chest and grabbed the pack with a many taloned paw and tipped it over. The O-ball fell out, inert and dark, and the creature poked at it with a talon. Seven gems lit up: gold, emerald, ruby, topaz, diamond, silvertine and orichaclc. The air smelled of cinnamon and coriander. It batted the O-ball with its paw and the ball stayed put. It swatted it with the other paw, failing to move the artifact. The jewels glowed.

The sarpanya shuffled up to me and blinked.

It huffed and reared up, spreading its scalloped bat wings, arms up, talons shining. Hyperventilating and dizzy, I looked for an escape.

"You want to play with this?" I laid my hand on the O-ball, which lit up. The crisscrossing rows of colored cubelets drifted in lazy arcs across each other. Light shone bright white like Altarsha's sun, but cool. Mesmerized, I forgot about the rock drake.

The air became exceeding chill, the lair quiet as a tomb. The rock drake froze its motion, still as a statue staring at the roof of the grotto, slitted pupils now wide ovals, stars reflected in them. Above me, strange constellations and galaxies shimmered with a slow turn of expanding suns.

I wished for a navcom link or data pad with a star atlas. My mother taught me math, not astronomy. Some of her songs spoke of ships sailing under dark skies. One line stuck in my head and I sang it low, my heart twisting as I pictured my mother teaching it to me. "What fate befell..." The words are in ancient Altari, and I spoke them without thinking. As I spoke the words, the chamber shook as if a hammer had struck three times. Steam vented from a wall and rocks fell from cracks in the ceiling. The sarpanya bellowed a roar. The projected constellations, and the o-ball went dark, everything dark. Caught I was in an earthquake, the only light coming from slitted glowing red eyes, and my torch casting a wan light under the pool's surface.

I snatched the torch, bruising my knees as the ground's shaking abated. By its light I retrieved the o-ball and stuffed it into the backpack. Looking up, I saw the beast's now red eyes blinking at me from one of the other exit tunnels.

By the light of the torch, it turned and slithered away in a silken rippling of scales and legs, its wings tucked flush to its body.

I wondered what would collapse first, the chamber or a tunnel. Being a stranger and alone here, I had little alternative but to follow my unlikely guide.

Time passed, but how much? My journey reduced to a shuffling, hunched gait alternating with scrambling up and down the tunnel, the sarpanya looking back at me and puffing steam from its nostrils and growling with a low rumble. I fell behind. Fatigue dragged at my feet. I sat against a rock.

My head ached and my arms stretched out as something tugged on my right leg, dragging me over gravel, pitch black darkness enveloped me.

"Hey!" I twisted and turned, trying to break free. My legs broke free, and the sarpanya loomed over me, staring at me with its luminous eyes. It reared up, spreading its wings, and roared.

I grabbed my backpack. The O-ball gone. The torch was still there, and I flipped it on casting a wan glow upon the beast in the immediate circle of light that petered out into inky darkness after a few feet.

"What did you do with it?" I shouted at my dubious guide. "It's all I got left of my family." I hit its shins with the handle of my torch.

It roared again, this time a wash of fire streamed overhead and its flames revealed ruins, ancient buildings, mausoleums or habitations. The O-ball sat on the ground, still and inert, a dozen meters beyond me, towards the buildings. Now that I knew where to look, I kept the torch on it, scrambling, as the fire stream abated and the shadows closed in again.

I clutched the ball in both hands, staring at it. The gems lit and the circling cubelets drifted. The shining lit the ground dimly.

"What no, projection? No fireworks. What the hell are you?"

I shook it in my hands.

"Answer me you, you..."

I sat on the ground holding the O-ball in my lap. "Who am I? What am I for?"

The sarpanya crossed over to me and sniffed at the o-ball. Then it curled up in front of me, wrapping its scaled tail around itself and me, and fell asleep. Terror had taken its toll and my best intentions failed to keep me awake. I dreamed of twisting steel and falling concrete, and my mother's songs.

9

Dark Waters

I awoke thirsty, my throat parched. I was alone again in the dark.

The torch had been on while I slept and now the light shone dim. Helpless and certain I would die here, I walked towards the largest cluster of building, with stairways switching back and forth to the floor of the enormous cavern.

A low wall bore an inscription in the archaic curl and bar script of ancient Altari. I knew many words and songs in the language thanks to my mother, but my mother had lacked written references to teach me the grammar of a language considered dead by most, and as I had learned, dangerous to some.

My captor had called the language proscribed, forbidden. I searched for old scrolls or books to read before my torch ran out, and I had to wait for a slow death.

One word on the stonework I recognized, the root word of the name my uncle rechristened me with. "Why uncle? Why *agni*?" With a sigh, I said the last word. A movement in the ruins attracted my eye.

Willowisp lights, dancing blades of yellow and orange, shimmering, winding from window to window. There were legends about the aliens who organized the galactic peace. There were rumors that the amari took varied shapes and any any appearance they chose. Pictures on walls with eyes that followed you, ghostly forms lighting distant towers on hidden islands, strange animal forms. The mirrors, equally uncanny, represented by the gems on the O-ball, as I called it, were the amari's gifts to the younger races to bind the galaxy together in a common peace.

Working myself into a cold sweat, I tried to distract myself. One gem seemed to match the shade of the lights, but this frightened me more.

Who am I? What am I for? I searched the walls for a clue to my name and found none. My torch was almost out of power. I switched it off and, tucking it and the o-ball into my back pack walked towards the ghostly lights.

I shied away from doorways and windows, searching for a semblance of staying outside, though buried under millions of tons of mountain. The lights confined themselves to walls and exterior structures. Nothing lit up the darkness inside the buildings. No sounds echoed but my own footfalls on cold stone

I tried another word of Altari, the ancient form. *"Asta"* Home.

The lights coalesced into an aurora of dancing flames on the roof of the vast cavern. A pinpoint of yellow light pulsed. There should be no wind. Lightning rippled across the roof and thunder boomed. Rain fell in drenching sheets into spreading pools that drowned the lower trail whence I had come and within minutes reached the threshold of the stairs. Sputtering and sneezing, I wiped my eyes and hair. Water covered my ankles. I retreated towards higher ground, closer to the stone houses with the shadow filled windows.

As I sheltered under a stone archway, the cavern transformed into an underwater lake roiling under sheet lightning. Plumes of water exploded into the air as from springs or geysers cut loose from their bonds. I ran into a gray doorway, the threshold dim with a wan light enough to see flagstones in a straight hall, a tiny square of light visible at its end.

The rising water pursued me and clutching my back pack I ran for the light.

Fast as I ran, the water rushed up behind me, a dozen yards behind when I got to an opening. Blue sky spread like a dome overhead, wispy traces of cirrus clouds, and the white heat of the sun beating on my face. An enormous tower rose from a spur of mountains in the distance, broad as a mountain itself at the base and ascending until I lost it in the blue above.

I looked down, perched on a cliff doorway, and deemed it possible to work my way down the slopes until I got to a series of rolling foothills above an enormous city spilling further down towards the giant harbor and vast floating platforms covered with cranes and factories and cylindrical and delta shaped constructs I recognized from my infatuation with Battlefleet lore. The floating shipyards of Ashastra Galactic, where the starships of the republic began their making, then boosted to high orbit to complete their assembly under the watchful eye of the paraman's base star and the home fleet.

Most of the buildings were skyscrapers, modern and packed tight on the upper terraces. Towards the water between them and the harbor sprawled the old city in a motley variety of styles and narrow streets except for the First Mother of the Republic, the paramani's palace grounds and the diplomatic compounds where the alien representatives to humans lived. I had seen plenty of pictures of aliens in books, but never met one, nor was I ever likely to meet one outside a big city.

Water poured at my feet. Gasping, I clutched at a bush to regain my balance. The water forced me onto the slopes. Clutching at rocks and shrubs to keep my footing, I barely made my way to a handhold before the water roared out and fell below, a new waterfall glistening in the sun.

The spectacular sight drew attention to my position that I did not want. A paroxysm of coughing shook me and a wave of nausea and fatigue followed. So much water and I had drunk none. Thirsty, my throat parched, I climbed down to the arid hills below.

10

GUILD HOUSE

Up in the northlands of my home world, there are fewer people. The mountain crags and pine forests give way to farmlands and the bigger towns. My journey underground skipped much of that terrain, surprised how I came 300 leagues in such a short time. Darkness underground and fear disoriented me.***

Still on foot, I traveled fast, running and jogging, yet it took a day to work down the steeper slope, just to get to the foothills. I drank from a creek with clear water that had an ashen taste. Taking only enough to take the edge off my thirst, I slept propped up in a royal spruce, hoping not to be eaten by a dendrapuma. I awoke to the sound of a turbo helicopter beating its rotors. A mile off I guessed it to be, and it shone a floodlight on the woods, passing up slope of me towards the new waterfall. Later, in the early morning, a sonic boom startled me and I almost fell off my perch. The orange haze of a multi-engine ship ascending into the sky. I guessed it must be military or it would have used the giant tower, the mercantile guild beanstalk for heavy lift and people traffic to low orbit. I couldn't sleep after that.

Driven by the fear that I might be caught and doing my best to follow my uncle's last instructions, I walked, hiding from casual passersby until I got close enough to Urbmar I couldn't do so without drawing suspicion. I feared a city prefect would wonder what a beat up looking boy like me was up to, but I didn't anticipate how little anyone in the city cared about random travelers, stray cats or boys.

Urbmar lay on the southern coast of the only continent of Altarsha. I had never seen so many buildings reaching for the sky, so many air cars coming to and fro, and up and down.

The city was ancient. I had no air car, so wandered alone through tight alleys. I searched for a merchant guild house, my last hope to.be come a merchant ship pilot someday. Interplanetary trade was as close as I would get to a starship, unless I found a powerful enough sponsor to intimidate or sweet talk a labor commissioner.

I was good with numbers and hoped to apprentice to a merchant that would take me on. I was just old enough to start indentured service. Once sponsored, I would be free to pursue my ambition. I hoped to earn a living while I studied mathematics. Eventually I might score high enough on entrance exams and get the attention of a Great House to sponsor me for pilot school.

I found a guild house for the interplanetary trade by a victory arch, celebrating the accession of House Ashastra to the emerald dais five hundred years ago. The broad, squat building contrasted with utilitarian dullness to the gold leaf and columns of the arch.

Passing indoors through a row of turnstyles, I asked the guard at the security desk for directions to the apprentice hall. He looked up and down at me and scowled.

"How long has it been since you washed, boy?"

"Don't know, sir, my parents would have boxed my ears for showing up like this except that they're dead." I glared at him.

"How old are you?"

"Fourteen, sir."

"Old enough to dig your own grave." He grumbled out the directions. "Present your ID or travel papers to the clerk and you'll get further instructions."

I almost walked out then, but I had few alternatives, and it was my uncle's wish I try. Perhaps he had friends here.

Clutching my back pack I passed through a security archway. An alarm sounded and a red light flashed. I walked on, pretending dazed stupidity.

"You there, boy. Stop."

Another guard diverted me to a customs table. A middle aged woman with worry wrinkles patted the table. "Back pack here." She scanned my body with a wand.

She opened the backpack. "What is this?" She held the o-ball, a dull looking gray-green octahedron.

"I don't know. My dad gave it to me to play with before he died." The tears at the corners of my eyes did not have to be faked.

"Ugly thing," she said. "Ah, here it is." She held up my last gold quant, the pure gold currency traders favored.

I stared.

"Weapons have to be checked in for storage, and all real money from unregistered visitors has to be declared."

"That's my last money. Are you going to steal it from me?"

"Watch your tongue or you can turn around and leave."

"Yes, ma'am."

"Name?"

I told her.

"Toragni? What family line is that?"

I shrugged.

She returned my items after logging my picture and entering the value of my 'real' money, and wave me on.

The apprentice hall, a long room with high ceilings divided space by Great House, six sections on each side with the adjudicator's office taking up the far wall met my regard with indifference. Lines of men, women, youth of different ages circulated. The entry way clerk asked me which house I was striking for work.

In truth, I had no idea how to choose.

"Ashastra Galactic has the juiciest jobs, House Santander the most dangerous, or," giving a conspiratorial wink, "possibly House Zayan if you go in for smuggling."

I pointed randomly at an emblem, a heron and lyre symbol.

"House Coriander? I didn't figure you for the artsy type."

He stamped a chit and motioned me forward.

One of my comic books told the story of the House Coriander champion, who had defeated a saurian gladiator in the Grand Arena. I didn't care about poetry as long as they could fight. I strode to their receiving desk, where a clerk in a voluminous blue robe and purple beret wrote on a parchment with a quill pen next to the computer keyboard. When he looked up, I realized it was an alien, the first one I had ever met in person.

It seemed friendly enough with its wide brown eyes, whiskered sea lion snout and dog ears, a harirossa. I knew a little about them from my mother. The Harry's loved poetry and music and ballads about conquering heroes or love unrequited. Mother had taught me a few of their songs. I thanked my luck.

It blinked and wrinkled its nose and went back to writing.

"Excuse me?"

"Yes, youth, found your tongue?"

"It's just that I've never actually met one of your kind."

"How scrupulous of you to admit that. I am Zanzibarminohar-larissanano, but you may call me Zan. How may I be of service to you?"

The end of the name told me it was a male. "I would like to apply for a pilot apprenticeship."

Zan sniffed. "Ah, poetry must wait." He set aside the parchment and tapped on his keyboard, looking at his monitor.

"Name."

I told him.

He looked up at me, eyes wide. "Why would your mother ever call you that?"

"What's so funny?"

"I will never understand humans, but Kiryan?"

"Zan, I need a job."

"Very well. Present your papers."

I shuffled and looked at my feet. "Well..."

"No papers, of course not. Human youth, for all they call you an adult."

"I still need a job."

Zan craned its neck and hiccuped. "Ah yes. Well, there's always biometrics." He pressed a button next to his quill and paper.

"What is the quill pen about?"

"It wouldn't interest you."

I hate it when people, aliens or not, are so dismissive. "I bet you are writing a poem."

"Hummpph."

"What do you think of Sarnashimastra's Ode to Beer?"

Zan's dog ears perked up. "Are you one of those drunks who mistakes art for an excuse for intoxication?"

"You prick me with your doubt. How about Zarathustra's Elegy on Starlit Dust?"

Zan shivered. "Once in a while I come across someone lettered. Who taught you?"

"My mother."

"Why is she not accompanying you? Ah. I see."

A human woman with a blaze of red across her short black hair and a nose ring accosted us. "Here, put your finger in the probe."

I complied, but she did not like whatever she read in her monocle HUD. "Bloody filtrig knockoff." She tested her own finger. "Umm."

Grabbing my hand, she tested me again, twice. "Zan, he doesn't register."

"Impossible, human assistant."

"Check the readings. His mitochondrial signature doesn't align with any archive records."

"But all you humans have a lineage."

I interrupted. "What are you saying? I had parents, I'm here."

She spit out the words. "Technically, you don't exist, or shouldn't."

The Altari Republic was powerful and ancient, and everyone had a purpose and everyone had a place, or they tended to disappear.

Zan frowned. "This requires an adjudication. No worries, human youth, they will check your chip."

There was a finality to the word that scared me. I had no desire to disappear or be anyone's prisoner again. Looking for the fastest way out, I scanned the room. It was only then that it registered. All the houses had sigil's and colors and one of them was orange and black. It had a broken stars and comet coat-of-arms. Another functionary at a desk similar to Zan's touched his ear and looked over in our direction, at me.

It was time to leave.

"Excuse me, Zan. Where is the rest room?"

"Really? Over there, and come right back."

"Yes, sir."

I cat stepped to the restroom door and kept on walking. Whatever suspicions I had raised, it didn't warrant an alarm, or whoever belonged to the orange and black wanted to keep things quiet.

Whatever happened, I would not go quietly into anyone's night.

I hastened to the street and ran.

11

CHANCE ENCOUNTERS

So much for plan A, uncle. Now what? I crisscrossed alleys and plazas with street vendors. After twenty minutes of evasive running, I sat panting in a doorway on a side street, sheltered for a moment from the white glare of the sun.

My mother was a Telluri. She was a commoner. My father was a minor house noble who married beneath his station into her line. But every human on Altarsha was descended from the original twelve houses of mankind and their mitochondrial DNA was the irrefutable evidence of their lineage. It just wasn't possible to turn up blank.

So who were the Telluri's? Was that my mother's real name anyway? The only family I knew was dead, and there was not even a DNA fingerprint to identify any relatives that might be mine.

The republic considered me a man, but without family, without sponsors, I could easily become a starving one. No labor commissioner would let me apprentice without identification. I would have to scrounge in the streets, become a thief or worse.

Like hell. There had to be another way.

After looking both ways and checking for street cams, I took the o-ball out. "Do you have a lineage?"

The gray green hue persisted, seemingly solid now, like a kickball waiting for action. In desperation, I risked another word. "*Jagrata.*" Wake up.

Nothing. So much for ancient Altari nonsense.

This was getting nowhere fast, and I was hungry. Putting the ball away, I ate one of my field rations.

Something furtive moved at the corner of my eye. When I looked, nothing. I caught sight of it on the second look, an insectoid figure twice my size. Forcing myself to be calm, I ventured the little Galactic I knew. "I come in peace. How may I assist you?"

The qondrotin alien shuffled forward on its six legs, looking like an overgrown combination of ant and praying mantis. I stood up, wanting to run, but you can't outrun a qondrotin, so that option was out.

"Do you have some food to share?" it clicked out in the trader pidgin of Altari..

I handed it a candy bar. "I hope you like chocolate."

"I am not a dog. Chocolate taste will not hurt me."

It gobbled up the bar with its mandibles, dripping brown goo. I tried to remember my manners and not throw up.

I dry heaved and my eyes teared up. "Pay no mind. Allergies."

"Ah, my thanks. Where are you bound?"

"Can you get me a job?"

"Would I be begging food if I could?"

"I don't know. Maybe."

Its mandibles clicked.

Qondrotins went in for hive thinking and an obtuse way of viewing human problems. "You didn't answer my question."

"Not I personally. Perhaps you could ship to one of our people's uranium mines. The pay is good, though I cannot vouch for your longevity."

"Safer to be a pirate."

"I can help you arrange that."

"Seriously?"

"Why would I jest with a human?"

I needed more time to think. "Where would I seek such employment?"

"Take my comm information and ask for..."

I could not fathom the clicks. "Pardon me." I pointed at my ears.

It chittered. "When in human land..." It offered me a business card with its comm address.

If I ever visited its home world, I might find employment there.

"If it's so hard for you here, why don't you go home?"

"I cannot admit failure of my project. Do you have another chocolate bar?"

A pair of police, a man and woman, in green and tan uniforms with black security vests rounded a corner up one block from us, walking towards us.

"You look pale, human. Why are you sweating?"

"Can we walk someplace?"

"Ah. The police are after you?"

"No, but."

"It's best not to be furtive around them. Your nobles feud above your heads, but they like to keep the street folk in order."

The pair neared us.

The woman of the pair looked up from their conversation at us. She motioned to her partner. "Jules, what do you think?"

He sighed. "Not all aliens are traffickers, Marta."

"He looks scared." She smiled at me. "Is this insectoid bothering you?"

"Uh. I was just lost, and I thought she might direct me."

The male police officer scanned the surroundings. I was not sure if he was bored or vigilant.

"What is your name, son?"

"Kiryan, ma'am." I coughed. I should have used a different name.

"Kiryan. Do you need my help?"

"Honestly, I need a job." I wove a story about my family's poverty, true since they were dead, and arriving in town looking to apprentice for work, any work.

The male police officer frowned and touched an ear piece. "There's been another gang fight at the harbor."

"Shut up, Jules."

"Just check their papers, Marta."

The qondrotin presented a data pad from somewhere on its carapace. Letters in galactic and common Altari marched down its face. She scanned it with a miniature signet wand.

"I hope your historical study of the Mirror of Flame goes well, professor."

"Wouldn't be caught near it myself," Jules said.

Marta held her hand out to me, palm up.

I looked at it, then up at her face.

"Papers, data pad, come on, child."

"I'm fourteen years old."

"Don't bristle so."

"Leave the little man alone, Marta."

"I lost my papers when I escaped my kidnapper."

"I'll scan your chip. Put out your arm."

I complied, first the right arm, then the left.

"I knew it. Someone must have pulled it to sell you on the black market. Don't be afraid. I can help you."

"Marta, you can't rescue every street rat in the city."

The qondrotin clicked its mandibles, asked if it could go, and with a nod from Jules, skittered off.

Marta summoned a lift on her comm. The robot taxi glided and the gull wing door popped open. "In with you, Kiryan, the taxi will take you to a social worker who can help you find your family."

"I can take a tram."

"This is better. Get in now."

"Am I under arrest?"

She rolled her eyes. "Of course not. But you need help, its written all over your face."

"Arrest me or let me go."

Jules smirked.

"Be that way. You are an unidentifiable vagabond, technically of age, and have the right to go, but not anonymously. Put your hand out."

"Marta, he's just a kid. Leave him alone."

"I'll tag him and he can go wherever he wants."

She didn't have a sidearm I could see, and her shoulder patch belonged to the municipal police, not the republican guard.

"Stop, boy!" Marta cried. Before she could say more I had sprinted away.

Scrambling as fast as I could, I heard no pursuit, and looked back to make sure. The robot car glided on silent magnetic fields pursuing me, its polarized windshield flashing bright red and blue. I squeezed into a space between two older buildings, not a proper alley, and barely enough to squeeze through. The car came up short and halted, nose yawing from side to side.

12

━ · ━

Crucible

I smelled salt air and heard sea gull cries. The harbor district. The old quarter would be busy, and evading through the winding narrow streets, I hoped to melt into the crowds. I didn't have a map. I was a stranger. Following my nose and my ears, I lost my way and ran into a rusty metal fence. A warehouse complex blocked my way. Automated rail cars trundled back and forth along parallel tracks. On the other side of the yard, sprawled clusters of run-down apartments.

A flock of seagulls passed over me towards that side towards dumpsters near one rail siding. I didn't see any guards. Automated cameras might see me, but maybe I could get across before anyone took notice. I scaled the fence and dropped to the other side, panting.

Winded, I had to slow my pace and walked across the graveled yard, timing sprints between passing rail cars.

A whistle shrilled. "You there."

I froze.

A grizzled man with a stubbly beard and weather wrinkled skin wearing a security guard uniform pointed a pistol at me. "Who are you and what's your business here, boy?"

My eyes searched the yard. In this open space I could not run, and I did not know if he was the kind of guard to shoot me or not. The seagulls had landed next to a half-open dumpster.

"You must be awfully hungry to trespass for that garbage."

"I guess I can't fool you, mister." I spoke in a low voice, eyes downcast.

He holstered his weapon. Grabbing his belt with both hands, he puffed out his chest. "Well, you won't rob anything here, not while I'm watching it."

"Can I go now? I just want to get to the harbor."

"Hell no. You're trespassing and I have to file a report. Now get going."

He motioned towards a small guardhouse at the end of a trestle crossing a ravine. He pushed me. "March!"

I trembled. "Please, mister. I didn't take anything. I didn't hurt anyone. Just let me go."

"Save your whining. You know what happens to trespassers, don't you?"

Actually, I didn't, having been schooled at home in the north country.

"I'll take you in and hand you over to the prefect, and you'll stay in jail until a judge decides what to do with you."

"No, please." I did not have to pretend my fear.

He smiled and nodded. "That's right, keep moving."

He had a gun and running might prove fatal. As we walked across the bridge, I saw the ravine was perhaps twenty feet deep and choked with thorn bushes and brambles. The guardhouse abutted an avenue that led to another gate and I saw shadows of people walking.

"Hurry up, I don't have all day. You look like a piece. The Guardia will figure out what to do with you."

I resorted to begging. "Please, mister, just let me go." My eyes teared up. He just grinned. "Shut up. Too many of you running around anyway, mucking things up for working folk."

I sagged my shoulders and trudged along. Then I sprang and snatched the pistol out of his holster and threw it into the ravine.

"Hey! Damn you, boy, I'll make you pay for that." He raised a fist to strike me. He was much bigger than me and I expected he could have hurt me if I grappled with him. I spun into a crescent kick and kicked his jaw, pushing him back. He grunted. Then I counter punched him in the gut. He bent over. Grabbing his belt, I flung him over the rail. He screamed and fell into the waiting thorns. Hoping he would survive, I ran for the street.

Once I made the road, I tried as hard as I could to blend into the throng. I looked over my shoulder every few minutes on the way to docks.

I ran for a plaza and hopped a public tram, the most crowded one I could find. I kept my eyes down and avoided talking to anyone. At the transfer station, I boarded a line toward the mercantile district at the base of the beanstalk where the house guilds lifted cargo to orbit. I came up short on the last leg, though, since the blue line required a fare. Exiting the station at the port district, I took stock of my situation.

The blue waters of the ocean rippled in the harsh white sun. Light danced on the waves, the smell of the salt air hung everywhere. Beyond the regular docks, taking up most of the vast Bay of Urbmar, lay the floating platforms for space ship construction, which only the nobility and Commonwealth military could access. The mercantile guild port was in orbit, and regular cargo rode up the beanstalk elevator anchored to the western peak overlooking the harbor.

The mass of human flesh and the occasional alien was punctuated now and then by animals, especially the feral cats that hunted rats near the piers for surface ships. Here and there ran scrawny packs of dogs, usually three or four, sniffing about and looking for scraps of food.

There were so many sights and sounds I marveled at that I forgot I was a boy alone in a strange city. My father would chide me for daydreaming when we sparred on the training mat.

My right heel itched. What the devil? I resisted the urge to pull my shoe off and scratch my foot.

A boot kicked me in the shoulder blades and plastered me to the cobblestones. I rolled to a sitting position.

Four boys, not much older than me, stood grinning. One had freckles and a pug nose. Another had disheveled brown hair and brown eyes that stared without expression, unforgettable eyes, eyes with no soul. Another boy, skinnier than the rest, hovered, wringing his hands about the orbit of the leader. The leader must have been sixteen. He was taller and brawnier than the rest, and out massed me by a good margin. Though my father had drilled me in martial arts since I could walk, it would be risky grapple with him.

I wiped the blood off my nose. I gave silent thanks my heel had stopped itching. I did not like the expression on their faces and would have to think fast. "Hey. Why'd you do that?"

The one with the soulless eyes jerked on my shirt collar and pulled me to my feet. Lightheaded and scared, I tried to back away, but they encircled me.

The ring leader smirked. What smugness in that expression. He sneered. "Dumb shit rube accent. What do you call yourself?"

"None of your business." Breathing hard, my fingertips and mouth tingled. Faint, mouth dry, my eyes darted, looking for an escape route, or help.

He chewed his lower lip and scowled. "You're from up north, aren't you?"

I looked at the waves to the south, past the trawlers and yachts. The edge of the space yard looked like a line of white against the horizon, wishing I could walk on water.

"Hey, fool." He puffed his chest out and his chin lifted. He pushed me, almost knocking me back down. "I asked where you're from."

I named a town. He had a mocking grin and a fevered look in his eyes that meant trouble.

"Search him. See if he has it."

The minion with the soulless eyes ripped my backpack off of me.

My heart twisted like a spring wound to breaking. I clenched my fists and widened my stance, facing quarter profile to him. He handed the pack to the leader, who rifled it.

I shifted my stance another step. He pulled out the o-ball. The eight sided spheroid with cubelets activated the colors and jewels shifting along their circular crisscrossing arcs.

He looked triumphant.

The skinny one almost capered. "We beat out the other runners." He looked around, eyes darting.

The leader ignored him and tossed the o-ball up and down. "What's this?"

"A hand puzzle my father gave me."

"What's it worth in trade?"

"I can't buy it back, if that's what you mean."

He laughed. "It's worth gold to me, unless you have enough to tempt me."I

The sycophant wrung his hands. "We got a deal. Don't try to wring water out of a stone."

"Who asked you?" He shoved the gangly one away.

"No one will give you much. It's broken."

He rotated some of the octagon cubelets, the colors mixed up. "Looks like it works to me."

"I was bringing it to a mechanic to fix it."

"Without money?"

"You shouldn't have taken it from the shielded pack. The nucleonic battery is leaking radiation and any second, the skin on your hands will start to melt."

He dropped the puzzle and everyone backed away. That gave me just enough maneuver room to scoop it up and tuck it under one arm to run. The soulless one shot out a leg fast as a snake and tripped me.

He pulled the o-ball out of my hands and handed it to his leader. I went to a half crouch, and I clenched my fists at my side.

He smiled and tossed the hand puzzle from hand to hand. "What'll you pay me?"

"Boss, she'll kill us if she finds out."

"You worry too much, Gecko."

He winked at me with a half smile. "I wasn't going to let him keep it, anyway."

I had no money. He would not have honored a bargain even to get my own back from him. My father had made me practice my forms as hard as my mother made me study math. It made me ashamed to want to hurt someone for any reason, but it was so.

"Give it back," I said.

He tossed the puzzle to his friends, who encircled me and passed it around. The others mocked me, laughing and snickering.

There are two kinds of power. One is the force of the fist, like space marines shooting pulser lasers. The other one is more subtle. From legends and songs my mother had taught me. Grief tore me at the remembrance.

I leapt to my feet, face hot, angry as a poked rock drake.

"Give what's mine back, you coward."

He over matched me in size and weight and pushed my chest with the puzzle. He forced me back a step. I grabbed at him, but someone pushed me and I stumbled. My face burned, my hands tingled. My right heel seared like molten glass.

The leader pushed me in the chest. "Try again, lizard meat." His friends grinned at the spectacle.

I had no chance to win a fair fight. Humiliation was better than a beating, or death, wasn't it? I should yield, grovel maybe. They'd leave me alone once they robbed me, wouldn't they? Maybe. But then I would have nothing to remember my parents by. I would feel as if I had let a bully kill them a second time.

There are two kinds of power. I faded into a back hand stance and surged forward with a spear hand thrust to the gang leader's solar plexus. A perfect strike might kill him. I did not want to kill anyone, so I pulled back at the last second. I was not a good enough kateka to fine tune it so. My arms and shoulders numbed after I jarred him.

I hummed a tune, and pebbles shook on the pavement. Then the soulless eyed one threw a hay maker at me and the blow to my head nearly knocked me out.

The melee began. I broke free and ran. I congratulated myself on setting a personal record for the hundred meter sprint. Something tackled me. Damn if it wasn't the skinny sycophant. The wind knocked out of me. They didn't even bother to pick me up this time.

The leader brandished a longshoreman's knife. "We'll drag him down that alley and cut his throat. Then we'll take his body to her for the bonus."

I shivered, and my hands sweated. New voices from behind me hissed and cawed. Something batted me aside. A dinosaur wearing a red vest and carrying a pulser carbine knocked the backpack from the leader and shrieked at him, mouth wide open with rows of teeth like daggers. The gang turned tail and ran away for what must have been a personal record for them, too.

13

THE SARPAN

A shadow loomed over me, blocking out the sun. My heart pounded and what little courage I had mustered in gang's face curled up into a little ball that sank into my stomach like a stone. An eight foot high saurian sarpan master, a sargon, bent down to examine me.

Of the various sapient species that made up the Commonwealth of Stars, the saurian sarpans were one of the oldest members and while I had heard of them and my father's stories warned of their ferocity and hunger for meat. They divided their species into biological castes, servants and soldiers stunted by genetic manipulation before birth, or engineered to be masters and rulers.

I had never any sarpan, much less a pack of the under class raptors that had surrounded me. What looked down at me now was one of tne of the sargons, the sarpan subspecies that acted as a combination of herder and sergeant for the raptors.

It carried no weapons and wore a service dress black and red kilt and tunic, with a serpent and golden scroll badge on its left shoulder. The alien sniffed at me, beady green and black eyes blinking. It bared its lips, showing matching fangs besides the serrated teeth.

I crab walked back as fast as I could. The city crowd streamed at a safe distance from the commotion. The sarpan pack surrounded me and I bumped into the scaled foot of one of the raptor soldiers who growled at me. I wondered why no constable was around to help me. Who let these aliens loose around here, anyway?

I looked up at the sargon. It bared its lips in a grimace I could not decipher and spoke in passable Altari."I am called Arkasa, diplomat to your world. Who are you?"

I shivered. The name told me it was female. I should have guessed. Females were larger than the males of the sargon caste.

"Do not fear, I have no taste for human meat, though others of my kind would differ."

"Um, I guess that's good." Nice to know the ambassador to humans doesn't fancy eating them. I stood up slowly, eyes darting for a gap in their ranks I might run through, if only I could snatch the back pack lying half to the side. The soldiers held small rifles, not that they needed them in close quarters.

Arkasa growled. The raptors shuffled and parted. "If you wish, you may go, but the next time you try martial arts on street vermin, make sure your body is equal to your bravery."

"Yeah, well." What could I say to that? "Thanks for being around."

"The city prefect would have found you eventually, though not alive. You are welcome. She handed my pack back to me. Where are your creche mates, or parents if you have none?"

I introduced myself and told her.

"Kiryan Toragni." She laughed with a wheezy gurgle that was difficult to tell from a snarl. Is she laughing at me?

"What's so funny?"

"Kiryan? You have such odd customs. Why did you come here?"

My parents had disciplined me by the Seven Precepts since birth, and I was reluctant to lie. "My parents died, and it forced me to run away."

"You seem to me braver to me than I would expect of a runaway. Come with me."

I hesitated.

She nodded and started off without me. The fear had worn off, and I realized what a fool I was. She claimed to be the ambassador to humans. And I knew for sure one thing: She was an alien and had traveled here on a starship.

"Wait, I'm coming."

I followed along. The raptor soldiers raced back and forth as they escorted us.

"They are restless," Arkasa said. "Too much time quartered for travel. The exercise will calm their nerves. Tell me, Kiryan." She laughed and recovered herself. "What is your heart's desire?"

I told her. I panted, huffing. Arkasa's stride was at least twice mine. "Where are we going?"

"To the paramani's palace, back to my compound. Matters of state await."

And what becomes of me? "Don't tell me. You are inviting me to dinner."

"Do you like pickled electric eels fried in suano blood? Or do you wish to be on the menu?"

"Er."

Another wheezy laugh. "Have you ever seen the palace?"

"I'm a commoner. They would arrest me for even crossing the Flame Gate."

"Not if you are in my company." She sniffed the air, bared her lips so her teeth showed. "The winds from the ship yards carry many scents.

What are you humans up to now?" She halted. "May it please you to let me see what you are carrying there?"

Her Altari accent was atrocious. I only knew a few words of Galactic, so I couldn't switch to that. Would she try to steal my puzzle? Not that it would do much good to fight a troop of sarpans. I handed it to her.

She turned it over in clawed hands; her forked tongue flicked at its surface. "The artificer made it of nov'argentum. The colors hide its nature. Do you know what these jeweled discs represent?"

"The mirrors of the amari."

"They are the eldest race, yes, and claim to have made the mirrors. There are eight sides to this puzzle but only seven gems. Do you know why?"

Was this a riddle, an IQ test? I shook my head.

"It is because there are seven mirrors of the amari. Why did you save it from the thieves? You might have outrun them."

"My father found it on a trading mission and gave it to me. My mother told me that if I ever solved the puzzle, I would be the greatest navigator the republic had seen in a thousand years."

This time, she did snarl. "Vain humans. And how is it solved?"

"When I align the eight gems to center on each of the matching side colors."

"An impossible puzzle."

"I'll settle for being the best starship pilot I can be."

"Of little use knowing how to fly if you do not know where you are going." Arkasa told me a little about the Commonwealth, about how each of the seven major home worlds had a mirror of the amari, how faster than light communication was only possible through the mirrors and it bound our civilization together. That much I had heard from my father, but not the proverb that followed. "Battlefleet keeps the peace, but the mirrors keep the soul."

I thought about asking her if she knew any merchants I could apprentice with so I could study my way into the guild exams when I was older.

"I know a few, but you should go to the guild halls for help."

"I tried that. According to them, I don't exist, or shouldn't."

"Yet here you are."

"Which is fine by me. All I want to do is be left alone and fly a trade ship. That would be enough to stay safe."

"You could stay safe, or seize the greater destiny that pursues you."

"I don't know how. Won't you help me?"

"Fight well and live, or not."

She turned away. How could I convince her I was worth her time?

"Is it true that a human champion beat a sarpan in single combat in the Grand Arena?"

She stopped in mid-step. Her raptor guards weren't the brightest, but they understood trade language well enough and bared their teeth at me, shuffling from side to side.

"You are lucky, Kiryan, that my duty requires diplomacy."

"I can't get a job without papers. I can't get papers without an identity chip. And I can't get an identity chip because my family isn't in the census data bank."

"You humans should worry less about lineage and more about your creche lord. I mean, your immediate clan leader."

"Maybe, but I'm stuck. You know our rules. How do I get out of this without my enemy finding me?"

"I must think about this. Walk with me to the palace."

The Flame Gate's splendor eclipsed the arch by the guild house.

Arkasa's tongue flicked. "The foundation of that wall was laid centuries before you learned space travel. It guards the Mirror of Flame."

"I've never seen noble house guards." Two armored hover carriers flanked the gate. Palace security in green and white field uniforms checked visitors through the gate itself.

"The troop carrier is the Battlefleet honor guard. Your young eyes would spark at the sight of their troopers in full power armor."

"You never told me about the human who beat the sarpan."

"Back to that, are we?"

"So it's true."

"Sometimes the bigger and stronger warrior is not the one who wins. I warned them not to try their gambit."

"Who?"

"A billion sapients watched that fight and you did not see it?"

"I think I wasn't born yet."

"It is easy to forget how short-lived you are. Factions within Sarpa wanted to conquer House Coriander colonies by using your own customs against you."

"What customs?"

"Your code duello, vendetta."

"I think a First Sister has a vendetta against me."

"The arena duel was a surprise to me, but your belief rivals it."

"I don't know why. But she killed my uncle by trying to kidnap me."

Arkasa snarled. "Where did this happen?"

"Can you get me into the palace service?"

"If a First Sister hunts you, how will you be safe there?"

"It takes a killer whale to stop a shark from eating you."

"Daring, and desperate. Consider those pillars/"

Made of a black rock, shiny as obsidian but stronger, the pillars to either side of the gate rose in spiral intertwined columns topped by stone capitals guilt in gold, and shaped to resemble flames rising from massive braziers. A bridge of stone lace work topping a broad metal arch damasked in copper and etched in gold with scenes from mankind's history arced between them. Pictures in video books did not do it justice.

Arkasa snorted. "Impressive, is it not for a race so young as yours?" Arkasa said.

I spied upon the frieze above, stylized ocean waves around an island with a mountain rising out of them and above a four-pointed star, the rays radiating out to a series of colored discs. They were the same color as the gems on my o-ball. The mountain had a Flëur-di-lis graven in its slopes, like the one on the brand on my heel.

"Youngling," Arkasa said.

"I don't belong here."

"Nor will you anywhere else in the same pattern of being. The paraman and paramani keep the Mirror of Flame here, as we do the Mirror of Lightning on Sarpa. Are you set on a plan? Will you enter with me and see what fate awaits you?"

Arkasa's raptor guard stood in two columns, waiting, fidgeting and growling. Their weapons were slung across their backs. An air car with a provincial governor flag glided past us, black and sleek as a python. Guards in white and gold uniforms, faces invisible behind mirrored visors on their helmets, passed it through. A house guard trooper with green and white livery of the First Family, House Ashastra, stood by looking bored, holding a beam rifle on a sling pointed at the ground.

Arkasa followed my glance. "What you do not see could hold off an army. And there is the House Ashastra Base Star overhead, watching always."

"I don't belong here."

"Youngling, you do not belong anywhere, but you might."

I looked at the Flëur-di-lis on the mountain and wondered. Sudden doubt. Uncle was right, I was a minnow swimming in a pool of sharks. "Why would you want to help me?"

"Let us believe I am irritated by your attacker hiding in shadows to strike at the weak. It seems in my empire's interest to discover why you would matter to one so powerful."

"How could I possibly help you discover that?"

"By working your way up into whatever fate lies written in your bones. Will you enter with me? I warn you, there will be no turning back."

I didn't have to stay in Urbmar. I had the business card and could call the qondrotin professor's associates.

Since I didn't exist in the database, I could just leave the city and forage in the provinces. I would be safe for a while, maybe disappear altogether. Become what? A pig farmer?

I ached to prove myself to parents dead. I ached to prove myself worthy of whatever purpose fate had slipped the o-ball to me for. There would never be a way to find justice for my uncle if I took the safer way, or answer the duty *bisnonn* tattooed my heel for. There was only one way to find out what it was anyway, to learn the purpose of my life if there were such a thing.

"I'll go."

Arkasa took me to a steward's foreman for House Ashastra, the ruling house not only of the planet but of the twelve home worlds of the Altari republic.

She bade me farewell. "If you must work your way up without family, you might as well start here. Better chances."

Altarsha was still my home world. My enemy was probably the paramani's enemy, too. "I'll be whoever I need to be for now."

No one would have given me a second thought on my own, but they let me in as an applicant on the recommendation that I had a warrior's heart and did they want to create an interstellar incident by insulting her? Besides her being in the diplomatic corps, it was hard for the foreman to ignore a sargon, even an unarmed one. Did I mention, the raptors bore stubby two handed carbines that shot hypervelocity darts? Palace security drifted around them like windblown leaves.

14

THE CHIEF STEWARD

The guards routed me to a gathering place where others my age striking for various apprentice shops had to meet interviewers for screening. I went for the math inclined and I got filtered into an office where we were given a two-hour test in basic math skills through first year graduate forms.

A dour woman in a gray skirt and fluffed out white blouse with a stylus stuck above her ear monitored the test. I turned mine in thirty minutes into it. She frowned and waved me off to another vestibule.

Sour faced testees joined me by the end of the two hours. The monitor dismissed us to the hostel to get cleaned up and rest up for the next day.

"Not you," she said to me, pulling her stylus out and pointing it at me. The others gone, the experience left me fearing another disaster.

She scanned my arms like the police did. Eyebrows arched. She shook her head. "Follow me."

I went down a side corridor, white paneled, white tiled with green accents, all looking the same. At oaken double doors with brass knobs, she knocked. The door opened soundlessly, one half moving just wide enough to admit me.

"Go on, she wants to see you."

There was nowhere to run. They trapped me.

"Impertinent street urchin, in with you." As she pushed me forward, the person I saw was not the one I was expecting. She was sitting cross-legged on satin cushions, facing a meditation pool with water lilies in the center of the room. The woman had long black hair almost down to her waist and wore a satin robe with herons embroidered onto the back and sleeves.

"Sit there, Kiryan. The door detected no weapons, so you can hold on to your pack for now."

Her desk was enormous with multiple banks of monitors and a small server farm glowing and blinking behind a haze gray window.

I sat on a matching cushion, cross-legged, breathing hard. Her limpid brown eyes smiled at me. "You are a mystery to me, and I do so like to solve mysteries."

"Ma'am?"

"Pick up that stylus and pad and solve the math problems as they present themselves. The tablet will adjust questions to your skill level."

"Who are you?" I blurted out.

"If I were a noble, you might pay dearly for that lip, but as it I am the paramani Ashastra's Chief Steward, Yolanda Hentanamira. She rose like a force of nature and glided to her desk, and took her seat, turning on a bank of monitors."

I stared.

"Wake up, Kiryan. To your work now."

A sense of familiarity with the exercise made time pass quickly.

"Enough," she said.

She had doffed her robe, and her business suit was the color of melted copper, a blue heron pin affixed to her collar. Her eyes remained kind, but I saw a tension in her posture. "What do we do with you, Kiryan?"

My throat tightened. It surprised me to find the backpack where I had set it down. I clutched it to my breast like a life vest.

"The police officer who tried to tag you filed a missing person report with the city prefect. A constable copied your photograph to the republic security directorate as an unregistered person of interest."

"I was minding my business."

"Then you show up on the door of the palace with the Sarpan Empire ambassador recommending you to palace service for your, and I quote her, 'doughtiness in combat'."

A servant wheeled in a cart and set two plates of sandwiches out, and orange juice on a table set up in front of her desk.

"Eat."

"Is this my last meal?"

"So cynical for one so young. I will taste the food first if that comforts you."

I was famished and attacked the plate set out for me. She ate her sandwich slowly and drank in slow sips, gazing at me the short time it took for me to eat.

"Kiryan, your math skills would rival that of a SciFleet cadet at Mahara."

"That's the nicest thing anyone has said to me since the last time someone tried to kill me."

"I am not a high noble to move people about like chess pieces and sacrifice who I will for my ambitions."

"Her tone was so like my mother's voice, all I could do was bow my head and look at the floor."

"Despite the law's opinion, you will not have the frontal lobe development for right judgment for at least ten years. You will perish unless you win friends or allies that can help you."

I suppressed a yawn.

"I will use Great House privilege to leave you free of an identifier chip. I am logging your mitochondrial DNA codex and sealing the record."

"Yes, mistress."

"Now you will tell me what you carry in your backpack that my door sensors say is empty."

What could I tell her? I was completely at her mercy. Bisnonn always worried. Always scowled and fumed at hidden perils. "I don't know what it is."

"Tell me what you know."

"Don't you want to see it?"

"I am not one to satisfy my curiosity without a purpose. Tell me first."

I told her everything except the part between the rock drake and my escape from the dead city.

"I sense you are telling me the truth. But what aren't you telling me? Show me this treasure that another house would risk vendetta with Ashastra."

I pulled the O-ball out, wondering what aspect of itself it would show.

Steward Hentanamira's eyes widened.

"My father called it the omegaoctahedron."

"I have never seen one before."

"You know what it is?"

"It is a toy the amari make for their children."

"Someone tried to kidnap me to who knows where for a toy?"

"What is a toy from their point of view may be something different for a human."

"The First Sister seemed to think it is worth killing people for."

Hentanamira called up databases on her monitor. Images scrolled, text in multiple languages, names of alien home worlds, including the amari capital world, Priamar. The information on it took up barely one page.

She sighed. "SciFleet archives at the galactic academy database at Mahara have record of one such device on loan for a research project studying trans-dimensional astrophysics. There are no pictures of it, and the amari ambassador repossessed it after the term of the research grant expired."

"Do you think this is the same ball?"

"I do not know. If it is, how did you father come to possess one?"

"Bisnonn sent him on a trading run. When he returned, he gave it to me as a gift, after she examined it."

Hentanamira frowned. "Your great grandmother acted like the matriarch of your family, yet you have no family line on record. What else can you tell me?"

No way was I going to tell her about my tattoo.

"So sad for one so young. You must store the device out of sight and mind or leave for the wilderness."

Boxed in again. When would I ever get the chance to live my life without interference? I had to trust someone, and I needed an ally strong enough to keep my enemies at bay until I was strong enough to take them on myself. Who was I kidding?

"If I give it to you for safekeeping, will you give it back when my term of service is up here?"

She nodded, a hurt look in her eyes. She was a commoner like me. I wondered if she was lonely, too. I gave her the pack.

15

—·—

RIOTTA

Hentanamira sent me to the head accounting steward, Ishi Riotta, a corpulent man with a gruff manner whose only answer was to grunt assent and wave me after him.

At a warren of offices well away from the main palace and diplomatic compounds, he assigned me a desk in a wide open space dotted with a hundred desks like mine, and men and women of various ages doing accounts, analyses and reports for the powers that employed us.

I learned the basics of bookkeeping quickly enough, and finagled my way into aggregating data from merchant shipping runs to the interstellar trade. Boring reams of ships' manifests and cargo transfers, marginal cost calculations, profit ledgers and insurance registrations which were a good proxy for what trade routes were most hazardous.

Pirate activity had spiked in the last two years, and the consular Battlefleet had increased patrols. Further information was unavailable, masked under security levels and need to know. Riotta docked me a week's pay for snooping those databases and told me two more offenses would get me transferred to scullery duty. He watched the log reports with a vengeance, and I plotted how to get access away from the office that he couldn't trace. I wished I could think of how to convince Hentanamira to grant me higher access.

I didn't know what I would look for, but my reprieve from enemy discovery could end any day without my even knowing it. Anger simmered in me, and I did my best not to let it fester.

I worked twelve-hour days for the next year. Not all those hours benefited my master. I pushed the memories of home away from me. The pain would drain me and then I would brood or be tempted to lash out in anger. My future depended on grinding out work until I grew old enough and strong enough to provide for myself. I could not waste it with a hasty word spoken in anger to a noble.

I redirected my pain to the gymnasium grounds, where I spent three hours every day practicing my forms. I took care to wear sparring slippers. The training gi's loose-fitting trousers hid most of the stars on my tattoo side calf. I masked them as best as I could with a skinshade ointment. I missed the O-ball and wondered where Hentanamira locked it up. Work and wait and gnaw on my inner demons seemed to be my fate. The tattoo could have been gone for all I felt it. The world seemed dry and all the colors washed out.

Other apprentices came and went, occasionally sparring with me. The dojo that the Ashastra sensei reserved for nobles forbade my entry. There were rumors among the steward apprentices that future champions of the republic trained there, like the one from Coriander that bested a sarpan in single combat. Republic custom limited that kind of champion to only one per house. The candidate filling the role depended on approval by a mirror of the amari. I had never met the Ashastra champion, and doubted I would ever travel in high enough social circles to do so, unless I earned a commission as a starship pilot in Battlefleet someday.

The gymnasium complex had a balcony ringing it on three sides. Restless after a workout one day, I found a solitary corner and watched the bustle of the city downslope towards the harbor. For now, I was safe from the cat that hunted me, a canary in a cage that belonged to a tiger with an appetite to protect its territory that liked the canary's singing — for now.

Surface ships plied their trade to other shores of the great continent that made up the main land mass of Altarsha, travelling up canals reserved for them, supplying the shipyard docks with material. The docks flickered with security screens that hid much of their work, the massive cranes jutting from them like flamingos above a mist shrouded estuary. Crashing white foam beat in marching lines from the blue ocean to the yards' seaward edge. My eye drew a line from the horizon to the beanstalk anchored on the right arm of the mountain range that formed one arc of the great harbor. White sparks glided up and down the construct, each a tram that might hold hundreds of people or tons of cargo.

The tower faded in the distance of layered atmospheric mists into the moonless blue sky. Legend had it that Altarsha had once had a moon, long gone since a forgotten cataclysm. The paraman's base star shone like a star in the deepening blue as the sun set westwards to my left.

At the zenith, where the dark held fully above the twilight, a shooting star announced like a herald, the free world beyond my gilded prison.

The next day, I sat in a cubicle working on the account reconciliation for Ashastra Galactic, the holding company for House Ashastra's trade and industrial projects. Riotta,the chief accounting steward and a corpulent man if ever there was one, assigned me the task. He planted a meaty hand on the desktop and leaned over me, his garlic breath distracting me as he watched my calculations. I took extra care not to miss a decimal point. The file reconciled properly.

He grunted and reached over me and tapped a key. The screen switched to my side project. I gulped.

"What is this?" he said.

"Linear algebra exercises." I didn't mention the partial differential equations or the great circle navigation problem.

Riotta hadn't risen to chief steward of the ruling house of mankind because he lacked intelligence. "This is not part of your work."

"No master."

"Your accounts have been correct so far. What use is this to you?"

I hid my ambition like a treasured gold quant I feared someone would steal. I shrugged.

He batted me upside my ear, though not hard enough to hurt. "Fool boy, you can make a name for yourself here without dreaming offworld adventures."

"Yes, sir." I swallowed acid taste. You can mock me, but you can't stop me. I had just taken the entrance exam for the mercantile pilot's guild. Thankfully, I had passed the first tier exam. A month later I had sat alone in my exam room for the second tier test, wondering who my rivals might be at other exam stations scattered across the continent, all striving for a coveted spot, so rare for commoners to gain.

Riotta huffed. "I know your family history. Why risk pirates killing you driving trade barges between planets?"

No matter how much I try to stop, I often suffer from my mouth talking ahead of my brain. "I want to be a starship pilot."

"A starship pilot? Who do you think you are?" He laughed until he turned red. At least it left him out of breath. My chest hurt as if he had stabbed me. I missed Hentanamira's kindness, and had not seen her but once since admission to the steward apprentice corps.

"Pay attention to your duties. There are others who would buy your contract."

Fear like a glacier weighed upon me. I looked back down at my accounts, clenching my jaw.

Riotta grunted. "I would already have sold you if not for..." His voice trailed off and I opened another accounting table.

After my shift ended, I spent an hour punching the makiwara board until my knuckles bled.

16

THE STEWARD HALL

The steward apprentices ate in a common dining hall. At lunch next day, I helped myself to a triple scoop of cheesed potatoes and enough fried game hen to feed a platoon. The cafeteria warden in the food line scowled at me and pushed an extra plate with broccoli and carrots, steamed, just the way I hated them. At least she didn't take my other plate back. I practiced my martial art forms daily with a vengeance and I would burn off the calories. Growing fast and ever hungry.

I sat down at an empty table feeling sorry for myself. Naturally, this attracted the notice of Jacobin Rentanamera, a steward of pots and pans and a constant irritant to me.

"Heya, Kiryan," he asked with a cloying smile that was his trademark, lips pressed tight like he was on the brink of an uncontainable barb directed at the nearest innocent bystander. "What's this about you wanting to be a starship pilot? Crazy rumor, no?" His eyes looked side to side.

I grunted, unwilling to give an answer, and shoveled a dollop of potatoes into my mouth. I pointed at my mouth as I chewed and shook my head.

Someone bounced into the chair next to Rentanamera.

Mistral Laghu was our age, fifteen going on sixteen years. Blonde curly hair, ice-blue eyes and a smile that dazzled me. She had loaded her tray up on gluten-free crisps, assorted braised vegetables, and a gelatinous square mass of soy protein. Her one concession to junk food was a chocolate malted ice shake. We had that much taste in common. Shy suddenly, I struggled with a different yearning. For a moment, I forgot all about starships and taunts.

"Hi Mistral." Lame, I'm lame. Don't be an idiot.

She had thrown Rentanamera's timing off. He nodded at her, eyes roaming over her figure with a hungry look. I attempted to look only at her face. I smiled, nodded, and hid my ineptness, scarfing down my food.

She giggled. "Kiri."

That was the diminutive of my name. "What's so funny?"

"Your name fits you." I would have thought she was taunting me, but she batted her eyelashes and sighed.

Rentanamera recovered himself and shattered the moment. "Heya, Mistral. Did you know he wants to be a starship pilot?"

"I didn't know you were that ambitious, Kiri. Aren't we lowborn good enough company for you?" She leaned into the table and my ears burned.

"Um. I don't think of it that way."

Rentanamera covered his mouth and stifled a grin.

She ignored him. "I will work up my way in state services and become an advocate or a diplomatic steward."

I nodded. "That's a fine goal." Twice idiot I am. Why can't I think?

"Maybe I can work my way into being a town magistrate, marry someone who will give me a big family, a baker maybe."

I couldn't follow her logic and stared.

"What do you really want to do someday, Kiri? Something you don't have to be a nobleman for?"

I had kept my eyes off her figure with a supreme effort, but it didn't do me much good. The twinkle in her eye as she bantered left me breathless.

"Mistral, if you keep that up, he'll bollix his presentation at the paraman's court."

"I'm sure he'll do just find. Won't you Kiri?"

My accounts were correct, but in my side studying I had completely forgotten about the Jubilee ceremonies and the need to practice my presentation. Steward apprentices rotated through court for one chance each to present their accounts to the paraman before final assignment to a court job or honorable discharge back to common life.

Mistral's eyebrows slanted down, and she pursed her lips. "Kiri, why are you so pale?"

Every third year, the paraman, the nephew of the First Mother of the ruling house of the republic, would hold a jubilee celebration and proclaim interdictions and give out favors, what we stewards called "dooms and boons" day. On this day, even a low born no account orphan like me could secure a favor, and I had already submitted my request, according to custom, in writing before I met the paraman. My odds of becoming a starship pilot without sponsorship would be nigh impossible. They assigned most commoners to the interplanetary trade. I had grown up on stories about the Commonwealth of Stars Battlefleet, but there was no chance of becoming a starship fighter pilot. It was the mercantile guild or nothing.

I had given up on trying to find my family, but I would be eternally grateful to Hentanamira for keeping the o-ball safe. My continued good luck depended on avoiding tracking chip implants and for that, I needed to satisfy my patron and keep his favor.

I stood, tray in hand. My forehead stiffened and my eyebrows wrinkled together. "Mistral. Jake." I strode off and tossed the remnants of my meal. There would be time to eat later, and i would use the edge of my hunger to prepare.

17

JUBILEE

The steward's companies stood arrayed at the left hand of the court, to the back of the golden hall near the five meter high bronze double doors rumored to have been the original doors of the first palace at the founding of the republic. The hall was large enough to hold several thousand persons. The limit depended on the mix of humans versus other aliens. I knew the exact count from the stewards' register, four thousand twenty-five souls present, of which thirty-six hundred were from the Great House delegations. This included stewards, adjutants, lords and ladies-in-waiting, personal bodyguards, and the dozen heirs and their near kin representing each house.

All the Great Houses had delegations present on Jubilee Day, and the ambassadors had turned out too, from the spindly insectoid qondrotins, to the seal like harirossa, and so on. I could see Arkasa, the sarpan ambassador that had befriended me on my arrival in Urbmar, and steered me to an apprenticeship in the palace. She stood near the paraman's dais and her saurian physique stood heads taller than any of the surrounding humans. A sarpan overlord would have towered over even her, but overlords left diplomacy to the sargon caste and seldom visited human worlds. Arkasa had only an adjutant with her. Most of her raptor guard remained quartered to avoid scaring the natives.

Among my fellow stewards, Rentanamera elbowed me.

I rolled my shoulder. "Shhh..."

He whispered, his voice partly covered by the drone of voices from the crowd of mixed human and alien dignitaries. "What are you going to ask for?"

"None of your business."

"I can guess."

"Guess as much as you like."

"I'm going to ask for a job in the capital as a sous chef."

I shuddered. "My condolences."

"Give it up, Kiryan. What makes you think you're so much better than the rest of us?"

The hall was lined with tapestries and statues marking the history and exploits of House Ashastra. Republican guards in blue and green uniforms studded with gold buttons with wide white sashes about their waists and wearing white gauntlets presented pulser rifles at parade rest. Their captain paced, eyes scanning the crowd, glance brushing past the stewards and other servants. He spoke into the microphone clipped to his epaulet. His HUD visor shimmered.

The Door Warden, in full green and white court robe and beret, carrying the warden's mace, a staff with a golden-winged sun emblem engraved with a silver door on the disc and silver rays spreading out, called the introductions as each dignitary processed up to greet the paraman or make a request. Sometimes these were threats. The sarpans considered it a matter of honor to deliver ultimatums face to face. Battlefleet kept the greater peace, but frontiers were wild places, easily prone to skirmishes and border wars. Two of the guards flanked the paraman, hands on service pistols at their side, looking stoney eyed at each human or alien that came before the paraman.

I stiffened when I heard my name called out. I wore a green and white groomsman jacket in the house colors, and dress knickers and shiny leather shoes, more like slippers with arabesque filigrees. In my poor planning, I had picked up too tight a pair from the quartermaster and so wore no socks. The uniform was adorned by nothing splendid, like a nobleman's armor, cape or technosword. I crushed the moths fluttering in my stomach and set my chin. My tablet of accounts was in order, fully charged. Clutching it to my chest like a shield, I walked up the center aisle for my one moment of fame.

I genuflected, then stood, head bowed, presenting the tablet files. My skin tingled with an odd sensation I had never encountered, a body shield field zone. The guards' expression remained masklike, their eyes fixed on me. "Your accounts, my lord, for House Ashastra in the last quarter."

Lord Karin Ashastra had the white hair common to his family and a youthful tanned face with dark brown eyes that had the intensity of a hawk. He wore flowing robes in green and white with blue slashes of color over a golden coat of chain mail made of orichalc, that rarest of alloys that made his armor alone worth a fortune.

The winged delta insignia on the wall behind him, a signet ring studded with emeralds, and a noble's sword sheathed at his side added to the intimidation factor. I held my breath. Then the lord smiled, and I my heart skipped and a wave of relief washed over me.

"I see our holdings have done well. Your steward speaks for your attention to detail."

"Thank you, my lord."

The paraman switched to Galactic. "Your application states you wish to remain in house service as a merchant pilot."

Doing my best, I answered with care. "It would grant me honor I do not deserve, lord, but it is so." Did I use the right Galactic syntax? Protocol rules spun my head in circles.

Switching back to Altari. "Not bad. Work on your language skills. A mercantile guild pilot runs into aliens often enough, I don't want to quell a war because of an ill-placed word."

"Where is your family, master Toragni?"

"I do not know and have no way to find out, my lord."

"My Chief Steward has a soft heart for orphans, but there are too many orphans for House Ashastra to sponsor them all."

Murmurs in the crowd rose. The paraman looked over my head. "We will speak more about this later." He nodded.

I touched my forehead with my right hand and bowed. I did an about face, and legs quivering, walked down the aisle flanked by aliens and dignitaries. I looked sidelong both ways, looking for orange and black livery, feeling too exposed.

I passed a crescent moon banner of another contingent of humans. A teenage girl about my age with long blonde hair, wearing a diamond studded silver tiara, caught my eye. She stood with the entourage of a Great House. My bitter self complained. Another noble, a princess, no doubt. She had fairer skin that belied coming from a planet with a sun less harsh than Altarsha's. Or maybe she just sits in her parlor ordering servants and never goes out. I had never seen anyone so beautiful.

Elation. Bitterness. I stumbled, righted myself and took my place, standing with the other stewards. Not yet full grown, I could not see above the older men and women in front of me. I sidled to one side, then to the other to get another look at the girl. Finally, a clear line of sight. Our eyes met. I gulped. She stared and did not flinch. Then a corner of her mouth turned up ever so slightly. My heart fluttered.

What did I want really? I should lie low, wheedle the paraman into merchant guild sponsorship and the privilege of staying untagged. That would be enough for safety. The O-ball could stay hidden as long as I needed to. That would be the safest route.

On the edge of escape to safety, my brown eyes stared into her blue ones. I suddenly felt I might want something more. Something too ambitious to contemplate. To secure the only way I knew how to give me hopes of ever approaching her.

Why was my heart pounding so? She covered her mouth with the back of one hand and smiling - or laughing? - turned away and whispered something to a not much older girl dressed in the blue and gray house colors, a chaperone? Helper? I know so little about her. My ears burned.

Something pushed my shoulder. Rentanamera again. "Look who's staring at the sky. Her name is Jenna ni Selene."

"OK." I shuffled to one side, both to get away from Rentanamera and hoping for another glance at Jenna.

He closed the space. "She's daughter of the First Mother of Selene. Good luck with that, moron."

Mixed emotions tightened my throat. I could not give an answer. My wit was too slow. Half an hour later, I would think of an answer.

A woman coughed. Mistral, two ranks over, cocked her head at me and smiled. Was I that bleeding obvious to everyone? Would someone hang a sign on my head with an arrow pointing at me for my still unknown enemy to see?

While I pondered this, emotions whipsawing like a coffee overdosed hummingbird, my chest tightened. Tingling arose in my hands and face. Rentanamera rubbed the back of his neck and looked around. The chief guard stiffened and his eyes scanned the room. My right heel pricked like fiery needles. Time seemed to slow like when I meditated in a half-trance trying to solve the impossible hand puzzle of the o-ball.

18

RAPTOR ATTACK

A sound of keening like a swarm of mosquitoes pierced the air. Light sparkled in flashes in front of the paraman. He rose from his chair, right hand reaching across his body for his sword. The two guards stepped as one in front of him. I saw faint ripples in the air where they stood, like desert heat seen at a distance.

More flashes of light. The curtain behind the paraman shredded. I felt shock, bewilderment. Shouts of consternation and gasps rose from the crowd.

A woman cried out on the other side of the aisle and she fell prone, a black dagger jutting from her back. A gap opened in the crowd as the surrounding people fled, trampling her in a stampede away from the thing that had appeared from the shadows between two of the tapestries.

A sarpan raptor, the soldier class I saw my first day in Urbmar. It lept into the aisle I had just vacated. Elongated snout, razor teeth, it hissed and snarled something in the sarpan language, which to me sounded like someone gargling with gravel. The weapon vest had no insignia, just black, shot with a red camouflage pattern. Oversized haunches with claws. Smaller upper limbs brandished a rifle that spat out rounds that keened whistling, aimed at the paraman's dais. I realized the sparkling light represented the rounds vaporizing as they impacted portable body shields.

The paraman stood and drew a sword which gleamed of golden metal that hummed; the edge brightening to a white light. Air like heat waves over desert sands roiled around him. The energy waves bleeding off it stroked my skin like a harp.

I trembled at the sight of a noble's sword drawn in anger. Something else rushed inside me at edge of my mind, like the deep awareness of trying to line up eight colored sides with all the center gems of my hand puzzle, or when a perfect punch landed and snapped a plank with force beyond my age.

I swallowed, my mouth dry. The raptor crouched, poised to leap, facing the dais. Body shields would not stop its momentum or its claws.

Arkasa roared. Imperious. The only raptor with her, wearing green and black livery, muttered and hissed into a comm. It had no weapons other than its claws. The intruding sarpan in the red camo vest ignored everything but the paraman in front of it.

Do something! Was that impulse for the others or for myself?

Everyone around me ran towards the hall doors, a mob pressing and flowing as too many tried to leave at once. The human guard platoon forced their way through the crowd, hampered by their panic. They could not reach the paraman's dais in time.

As the raptor crouched and its haunch muscles tensed, a small box clipped to the raptor's vest sparked and exploded like a firecracker. The air transformed to greater clarity. It had a body shield, too. I looked in the direction from which the shot had come.

Next to Jenna stood a man in civilian court dress complete with a ruffled shirt and double-breasted waistcoat. He aimed his pistol at the raptor. It whirled to face the Selenite guard. Snarling, it bounded in a

ten-foot leap and as it landed squarely in front of him, bit his throat
out with its fangs. He dropped headless, and the gun tumbled from
his dead hand. The girl with Jenna screamed and fainted.

Anxiety clutched my chest for Jenna, and I ran towards her, stoop-
ing and hoping to run behind the raptor and not be shot for my
trouble. Jenna tucked and rolled, coming up with the dead guard's
pistol in a two handed stance and fired twice in succession, grazing
the raptor's left shoulder. The raptor kicked at her with its right foot,
the dew claw swiping the air like a scythe forcing her to retreat. Off
balance, she reached back to the side with her right arm to steady
herself, and lost her grip on the pistol, which fell to the deck. The
raptor kicked it out of reach. Backing against a pillar, she moved with
a measured alertness that awed me.

No. No. I can't bear it. I ran at the raptor. It sniffed and turned
towards me, jaws snapping. I juked towards a tapestry and jumped,
holding on, pushing into an arc that brought my feet to its snout.
Kicking hard, I connected and lost my bloody useless slippers.

It shook its head and sneezed. I ducked under its jaws. My father
had drilled me in his martial arts since before I could walk. Hand to
hand fighting was one thing. Hand to claw? Not so good. I did my best.
I channeled my fear into anger. Control. Control. Mind like moon.
Mind like water. Time slowed. The formless awareness at the edge of
my mind stilled, but I could not keep my inner pain from steaming
the water. I was on death ground. I met the raptor's charge. It was too
strong for me to parry. I back stance retreated, trying to lead it into a
clear field of fire, away from Jenna.

I could not dodge fast enough. A claw drew a line of blood as it
dragged along my left forearm. I round house kicked its head, striking
it in the temple. My fists were too feeble. I relied on speed and kicks.
Our duel turned into a kind of macabre dance as bloodlust drove it

to kill me with tooth and claw. My calves burned. My breath came in gasps. I just wanted enough time to distract it until one of the real guards could take it down. Why wouldn't they shoot it? The paraman motioned his bodyguards back, staring at me. What is this, an arena spectacle?

Out of the corner of my eye, I saw Jenna reaching towards the floor to retrieve her gun.

The alien backed away, swinging its head from side to side and shook its rifle at me, opened its mouth wide to roar defiance. Damned if I would die without making it choke on my blood. I scooped up one of my lost slippers and as it lept to crush me, I dodged as the sarpan tried to bite my neck and I threw the slipper down its throat, almost losing my hand doing it. It gagged and staggered. I backed away slowly, keeping myself between it and Jenna. "Get down, you peon," she said.

The sarpan belched out the slipper in a roaring shriek. I ducked to one side and saw Jenna take aim to fire, but the raptor whipped her jaw with the butt end of its rifle and sent her sprawling. She lay still.

Searching for another weapon and cursing palace security under my breath, I picked up an ornamental bronze urn. Gods the thing was heavy, and swung it two handed and heaved. It landed on the raptor's right ankle. It stumbled and shook its foot free. Snarling, it pointed the muzzle of the flechette gun at me. I faced straight down the barrel with nowhere to run and out of ideas. A strange peace descended on me. I had done what I could. A blur of light pulled me back into the moment. A luminous sword cleaved the lizard's neck. The raptor collapsed, twitching. Other guards ringed it as it died.

The paraman's blade stopped shining, no trace of blood on it, and he sheathed it. I hyperventilated, lightheaded. Worry gnawed at me. I had failed to save anyone. Nausea rose like a black wave as I thought of Jenna laid out on the floor by the assassin. The world closed down into a tunnel on me and all went dark.

I awoke, dazed. Jenna looked down at me, worry in her eyes. She had lost her tiara in the brawl and her coiffed hair, freed of its bonds, framed her face in a corona of blonde glory draped over her bare shoulders. Beautiful. A bruised welt showed on the right side of her jaw, but she was alive.

I sighed and smiled. "Good."

The paraman stood by silent. His glance roamed over me. A medic knelt beside me, bandaging the wound on my forearm. The paraman stared at my right heel, the heel with the tattoo, the Flëur-di-lis and dragon flying over ocean waves. His expression froze like a stone mask.

A guard captain helped me to my feet. The paraman lifted my chin with his right hand and stared at me. "So you are the scribe with a warrior's heart. I did not believe her."

"Sir?"

"Arrest him."

The guard captain hesitated at what must seem like an odd order for someone who had tried to foil an assassination attempt. The paraman glared at the guard, who bowed his head and brought the side of his right hand to his chest and chopped downwards in salute. Two guards held me and led me away, barefoot in chains.

19

DUNGEON

They marched me down to a section of the palace grounds where they kept prisoners. A scullery steward described it to me once as not being much to look at. She would deliver a cart of meals to a warren of white-walled halls leading to holding cells that looked just as sterile with bored prisoners playing card games or watching reruns of arena contests.

I kept looking for which cell the guards would deposit me in, but we passed the halls to a stainless steel door that whisked open into an elevator. The guard thumbed a scanner, and my stomach dropped as we fell for minutes.

"I thought we were going to the paraman's dungeon?" I ventured to say. The only answer I got was a sardonic "And so you are," from the sergeant.

When we stopped, the doors opened to a dank stone corridor with lichen hanging from the cracks in the ceiling. As they marched me forward, I could only see about ten feet at a time into the wet silence, walking on cobblestones cracked and blistered, with flakes sticking to their surface like old leaves. Electric torches lit at intervals in sequence and blacked out behind us as we passed. The hall branched five ways, and I saw blocky wooden doors crusted with rust stains from iron-barred windows whose glass sagged in ripples. I heard pounding on one door as we passed by, muffled, and imagined I heard a man's voice, weak and pleading.

"Are you going to kill me?" I asked the guard.

"No lad. We're more civilized than that," he said.

There's no capital punishment in the republic, except for high treason. I had never heard about this part of the paraman's dungeon. I wondered if that was because no one who entered ever left.

They put me in my cell. Dark basalt walls stained with moisture and rust-colored streaks where there were no iron bars. A straw mat in the corner, a chamber pot in the opposite corner, spitting distance if I had any tobacco to chew. They unshackled me and locked me in. All I could see by was a dim glow bulb, amber just bright enough to cast my shadow on the wall as my only company.

What had I done to deserve this?

I don't know how much time passed. I was still too young to gauge it by my beard's growth. They fed me at intervals, gruel at one time, fruit and meat the second time. Using them to guess the passage of time, two meals a day, I went through thirteen pairs of meals when one morning or evening; the door grated open, and a seneschal entered. I could tell it was a seneschal because her white and green court robe only reached to her knees and she wore a silvered chain mail coat under it. She carried a golden mace with the winged delta sigil of House Ashastra. She frowned at me. I thought she might brain me with the mace, but she waved it to the door, and two palace guards dressed in white and gold uniforms with epaulets dragged me to my feet. I shrugged my shoulders free and glared in return.

We retraced our steps, I thought, to another steel door like the lift that had dropped me here. The place was a maze, and the seneschal's mace glowed, waxing and waning as she turned it back and forth. A homing beacon, I guessed. A way out?

I considered wresting it from her and making a run, but where to?

"Don't even think about it," she said.

"What? Me?" I did not know what made me such a threat to interstellar security. She would assume I would try running for it.

"You would never find your way out."

"What about your homing mace?"

"They keyed it to my mitochondrial DNA. Unless you are high in House Ashastra's genealogy, you can make no use of it."

"How are you so sure I'm not?" Nobody knew my family line. Perhaps I would confuse the mace and it would let me use it, or zap me dead for an impostor.

She laughed at me. "You should be so lucky."

Mulling this over, I followed her into an elevator, still flanked by the guards. I knew enough about palace protocol to recognize their uniforms as a special guard unit, but attached to whom?

The elevator rose an interminably long time. Was it my nerves, or was this taking longer than the first ride down?

I kept wondering when the doors opened to a fluorescent white light and a long hallway.

I followed the seneschal, flanked by guards, through a series of corridors unlike the dungeon. The first lined in white tile. They forced me into a room with a padded chair with a footrest and headrest. Are they going to torture me?

They manacled me to the chair and a wisp of a man came in with scissors and a comb.

"Make him presentable," the seneschal said. She left with the guards. After shampooing my hair and doing a haircut in total silence, another attendant entered, a man of similar demeanor but much larger than the barber and me, with a eunuch's earring. He unshackled me, then gripped my shoulder with hands that felt like they could crush me, stripped me, dragged me into an adjoining room lined with tile and threw me bodily into a shower where near-scalding water doused me.

"Dress in the clothes provided when you are done."

He left me mystified. Clothes lay on a stool — nothing fancy, just apprentice breeches and shirt, and wooden clogs with scratchy woolen socks.

When I reentered the barber's shop, the seneschal and guards were waiting for me. I followed the seneschal into a second hallway, this one tiled in green and white jade, then into a third damasked in gold that looked like a museum hall, with suits of armor and weapons from the centuries past lining it. The ancientry and majesty of House Ashastra beat down on me. This is the family that rules the stars.

It ushered me out the last door into the last place I expected.

20

THE PARAMANI

I blinked, unused to it, and saw a bright blue sky above and heard banners fluttering.

I entered a wide pavilion lush with tropical plants and fountains. An arc of flagpoles with pennants of all the Great Houses rose above and behind me.

I hesitated. From my briefings in the stewards' hall, I knew I was two hundred stories above the summit of the tableland rising from Urbmar harbor. The seneschal bowed and retreated into the elevator. The two guards escorted me up an aisle with a blue carpet flanked by statues that looked like rock giants out of legend. Light curled and sparked across their gauntlets and pikes, and I realized they weren't statues, but Battlefleet star troopers. Their shoulder insignia bore the winged delta sigil of House Ashastra. The pikes hummed with a resonance that reminded me of Lord Ashastra's sword when he had drawn it.

Who rated this kind of security? I flinched inside at the answer that came to mind.

At the end of the carpet, sitting on a low wooden chair framed by drapes of green, white and gold, sat a white-haired woman. She wore a long green gown. A white cloak with an emerald and gold brooch. Strong hands folded in her lap reminded me of my mother. They were hands that had seen work.

A guard pushed me to my knees. I did not resist. They had brought me to the First Mother of House Ashastra, the aunt of the paraman, herself the most powerful human in the galaxy. I stammered, trying to speak clearly in Galactic. "Your grace. Reverend mother." I looked at the floor, noting the fine weave of the carpet and feeling very small.

"They tell me you are only fifteen years old and you fought a raptor, unarmed."

"I, I..." What could I say? The enormity of who she was compelled me to silence.

"It is difficult to be a child becoming a man. You have made a good start."

"Then why did you have me imprisoned?" I left out her title. Maybe a mistake, but my emotions whipsawed into burning ire. I wished for a tzaka board. I quelled my anger. "Reverend Mother?"

"Your Galactic is passable, Master Firehill. Tell me why you risked your life in such a foolish manner."

I lifted my eyes. Was that a trace of a smile on her lips? "I could not help myself. I had to."

"No one has to do anything, yet you braved near certain death. Why?"

She was a mother in more than a political sense. I was so lonely. I stifled the feeling and choked out an answer. "To save a woman."

"As simple as that. I wish I were young again to feel such urgency to love. My husband was the same as you when we first met. Alas, he is gone, and there are so few left among us with such a pure heart."

My knees ached. I fidgeted. Why did you jail me?

She smiled. Motioning to an attendant three paces away, standing with head bowed and hands folded. "Bring the young master a chair and let him sit so we may talk awhile."

She had given me a singular honor. The attendant rushed in haste to comply, while the guard's mouth hung open, then he shut it. The attendant proffered a chair, set in the center of the carpet facing the First Mother, the paramani.

I sat. My feet barely touched the carpet, as if I were a small child, legs dangling, nervous on his first day at school.

"That's better. Bravery is its own reward. I am sorry for your inconvenience. I hope you do not think to expect more of her."

"Is that why you jailed me?"

She frowned. "The girl you fought for is too far in rank above you. A youth like you might think of hopes that are best left to wither on the field. But that is not why my son imprisoned you."

I blinked. I could not deny my admiration of Jenna's mettle in the face of death. And she was beautiful, too.

The paramani frowned. "You are a sparrow flying towards the sun. You can only burn up and fall to your death."

Even now, I am impetuous. As a fifteen-year-old, goaded by such a remark? "I will fight for her hand."

"Bravely said. How will you convince her family to let you approach her?"

My chest tightened. I stared at the ground. My thoughts froze. Shenna called me a peon.

"Noble house marriages, especially Great Houses, are always arranged. Her family will pick for her from a suitor they approve."

"Does she have any say in it?"

"Of course she does, child. But she will only choose from among those her family thinks worthy of her."

"Then I will have to become worthy." Why should I not have a choice? Why should she not?

"You would have to be raised to the peerage, a knight at the minimum, if your military exploits justified such regard. What is your plan?"

I knew then it wasn't enough anymore to become a merchant guild pilot. Why not? It's what I always wanted to do, anyway. "I will have to become a starship pilot with the Commonwealth Battlefleet."

"A fine trick, since our realm's rules only permit nobles to apply for those positions. I draw even the privates and sailors from the minor house nobility. You would have to be a savant or a prodigy. It is not enough to be a brave fighter."

"Ma'am?"

"Humans are the youngest members of a galactic commonwealth made up of older races who still regard us as inferior. You have heard the sarpan term?"

Arkasa had been the only sarpan I had ever spoken with. I shook my head.

"Clever monkeys. That is what they call us, as if we are little more than animals." That was when I first learned of their biological caste system.

"Your face reflects your horror, yet it is so. They mold their young without pity. The upper caste is proud, and they style themselves as an empire. If the amari and the other races did not keep the peace with the help of Battlefleet, the sarpans would try to conquer us."

Being a steward of accounts made me privy to the amount of money House Ashastra spent on weapons research. They were into some truly epic hardware. "We would win, right?"

She sighed. "That depends. The people and ships we contribute to the Commonwealth are some of its finest troops, and who can say what secrets we keep for ourselves? We would bloody them. We might win, but at what cost?"

"You will always need the best starship pilots."

"You are a persistent boy, aren't you?"

"Tell me how I may earn a place in Battlefleet."

She waved the request aside. She shivered. "Forgive me, child. You are thinking only of your heart. I must worry about billions. I must decide now whether to let you live."

21

INTERROGATION

I chafed at the shocking threat. Stood. Clenched my fists. Legs slightly bent at the knees. We are two hundred stories above sea level.

The paramani cleared her throat. One trooper walked over. The silence of his approach surprised me. Battlefleet armor had suppression fields that would do such. A white-gold faceplate faced down to me from above, and an armored gauntlet grabbed my shoulder, fixing me to where I stood.

She really might kill me. What do I do now?

The paramani continued in Galactic. "An animal would gnaw its leg off to escape the chain, young Firehill. Are you such?"

I could not resist glowering at her, but remained silent.

"The paraman imprisoned you because of the sign tattooed on your heel. We have seen no one dare to wear that sign in an age. If you wear it without sufficient cause, you will die."

"It would seem you would hurt the innocent. What if a sailor got that tattoo, not knowing better?"

"The image is too authentic for such a coincidence in ways you cannot understand."

"My great-grandmother tattooed my heel the day after her husband died. That's all I know."

"Even if you have a right to wear it, the few who know its meaning would see you dead for it."

To hell with protocol. "I may be just a useless peasant to you, but I tried to save a princess' life, in case you forgot."

"Sergeant Major, draw blade."

A buzzing sensation assailed the corner of my neck. I could feel the wash of the heat from the glowing knife brandished at me. I leaned into it and turned my left foot out.

"Do not try that form. It will only get you killed."

I froze. Evidently, my father wasn't the only one who recognized the martial art he had taught me.

"I will recite a fragment of a poem in Altari. Some call it a prophecy. Then I will allow you one question before I decide your fate.

"Sacate anivirita vaniksaksikam…"

The paramani waited, the blade tingling my neck above my jugular vein. Sorrow overcame anger, leavened by fear. What question could I ask that would save my life?

She had switched out of Galactic into the same ancient form of Altari my mother taught me. I remembered a melody my mother sang it to when I was a toddler, before death entered my family and changed my world. From a well of memory, I heard her voice rise to the surface of my mind like a bubble. Seek the way that was lost. The words were too old for me at the time, and I never understood them, but I remembered them and the refrain within the song.

The paramani asked me a riddle with a trap. I would ask none of the myriad questions of my sorrow and dismay, but would answer her literally and trust my fate to my mother's words.

I answered in the same language. "What fate encompassed our high prowed ships at the coming of the serpent in the night?"

She nodded. The trooper sheathed the blade. "That is enough to tell me you are not an impostor."

"What if my mother was an imposter and taught me the right words?"

It would be better if we could match your mitochondrial DNA print, but it is not your fault those records are lost."

"What am I then?"

"It is better that you not know what you might be. If I followed tradition, you would not leave this room alive."

"But?"

"You had the highest score in the mercantile guild pilot entrance examination ever recorded. You may recall you had to take the test again?"

"I thought it was just the next tier of the exams."

"Yes, created just for you. The masters could not believe the score and were sure you had cheated. They observed you with a spy bot and recordings in a security grid cage room built to ensure you had no way to cheat, even if you had a neural implant, which you don't."

"So, what will you do with me now?"

"A mind like yours could be useful to us. There is only one way for us to let you live. You must go to Mahara."

All my scheming and anxiety had not dreamed of such a favor, yet coming from one that had no qualms about executing me for no fault of my own alarmed me.

Mahara was the joint services academy for the Commonwealth of Stars. Anyone who served a career with distinction had a chance at promotion in social rank. He might even marry a princess someday.

"We will sponsor your schooling. You did your best to help the paraman, even if it was only to save Jenna."

Riotta had taught me many things as an accounting steward. "What is your price for letting me go to Mahara?"

She nodded, a thin smile, then lifted her chin in an appraising look. "House Ashastra will sponsor you and hold your fealty directly to us. I will black out your tattoo out and you will never speak of it to anyone without my leave, or my successor if you live that long. Do you agree?"

Cornered. Would I start my career in the Commonwealth Battlefleet with a lie? "Do not mark me with shame by covering the only memory of my family."

"We are not giving you a choice."

"You just told me no one ever has to do anything. I refuse."

"Then you will die."

Nobles put great stock in their lineage. I wept inside for my family. How could I deny them and dishonor their memory? I took a chance the paramani would understand. "If you take my family from me, what is life to me?"

She frowned, muttering something under her breath. "Very well. We will grant you your wish."

Relief.

"Guard, kill him."

22

ETTIRKA

As the trooper lifted his blade, his grip shifted on my shoulder, and the gauntlet relaxed. Not enough to escape. He forced me to my knees and pulled my head back, exposing my throat. I squirmed and twisted, but the armored gauntlet held me too tight. Anger roiled inside, then a bleak resignation. Then a word remembered, like a cold dash of water to my face.

Etirrka. Resist. My right heel burned; something hissed in my ear.

They had not bothered to tie my hands. As the trooper brought the blade down to cut my throat. I reached up with both hands and grabbed his knife hand by the wrist. The blade's descent arrested, and my forearm muscles bunched and burned.

A faint whine hummed from the suit, and the blade inched closer.

Etirrka.

Connected to I knew not what, the center of the world low in my gut, time slowed. I imagined the trooper to be a tzaka board. I recalled the sensation of training to break it in two. Imminent death focused my mind, anguish at the loss of my family, anger at the injustice of dying for no crime I had committed other than being born.

I let out the word like the shout at the end of a fist strike — like the shout from the center of my core when I broke the tzaka board.

ETTIRKA!

I flung the trooper off me, catapulting him in a flying cartwheel arcing in a trajectory that took him over the parapet. I didn't mean to do that. I never wanted to hurt anybody. One time when I was ten years old, I found my cat playing with a mouse in my backyard. But it would not kill the mouse. I got annoyed and picked up a shovel and killed the mouse. The little thing stiffened in death. The cat looked up at me with eyes as if to say, why did you kill it? We were only playing. I hated myself for a month after that. And now I had killed a man.

From the edge of the roof, he returned, rising like a warbot and coasting on anti-gravity boots towards me. Though relieved I had killed no one, I dreaded his approach, floating towards me with that shining white knife to carry out my sentence.

I dropped and rolled. The only chance to live lay in escape, not combat.

I was about to die. I knew I would never ascend to anything. But neither did I betray my family. Was it worth it?

I never had a chance. Not at these odds. No matter what my mother's songs promised. Not unless I knew how to fly. And where would I go? I dodged and evaded as long as I could. Until too exhausted to take another step. Inexorable armored gauntlets lifted me like prey.

I panted, sweat-drenched, a rabbit trapped by foxes. The paramani's eyes were wide with astonishment. Two troopers flanked me, holding each of my arms as I stood on my feet facing her. A third held a pulser pistol barrel against the back of my neck. A fourth stood before me, facing the paramani, holding another luminous knife up in the air, ready in a salute.

I almost passed out. I gasped for breath.

"Brave, but foolish. Your service until now has been impeccable, and the record shows you resisted more than one bribe attempt from merchants and our agents. Your fealty would have been worth much to me."

I thought I knew how nobles thought about these things. "What good is my fealty to you if I betray my family's memory?"

She understood too well. "What words do you wish to be your last?"

"Did it occur to you that my mother might have taught me other songs you don't know?"

Her expression froze. "Are you threatening me?"

Oops. "No, Reverend Mother. But if you kill me, what else will you lose?"

"A cunning heart and a brave one. Do you have any suggestions?"

I did indeed.

We struck a bargain. I would submit to a superficial masking of the tattoo, which I would keep hidden unless bound by honor and duty to reveal it. Altari are sticklers for details in matters of high justice, honor and duty. I would worry about that detail when the time came. There was another consequence to our bargain I had not expected.

The paramani smoothed her skirt out with her hands and raised her eyes to mine in a level regard. "When you go to Mahara, if you pass your preliminary studies, the Mirror of Waters will test you."

"I don't understand."

"You are a commoner of uncommon danger to the republic. To enroll in the academy, you must pass an ordeal at the dharanadarza. Do you accept this condition?"

The Mirror of Waters. It was the mirror of the amari stationed at Mahara, the common heritage of all the sapient species. "I'm human. Shouldn't I be tested on the Mirror of Flame first?"

"Your chances of surviving the agniadarza without more preparation would be very low. Consider it a favor that I will let you defer your ordeal for now."

"Even if you pass the mirror's test at Mahara, your trials will only have begun. Do not deceive yourself about your chances. Most heroes are made, not born. The paraman has had a lifetime of training. When he marries, the woman who will be the mother of the next First Mother of the republic will also have been trained. Jenna is like that. She is strong, but I fear not gentle. Winning her would disappoint you."

I stifled my retort at her presuming what would make me happy. "I will do my best, paramani."

"Ever so rarely, in years counted by centuries, a hero is born who can ascend to the heights from the depths of his circumstances. I will give you a chance to do so. But I warn you to be careful about the reasons for your ambition and the pride that will shun the help of people you deem less than you because they did not strive for so high a mark. If you fly too close to the sun without their help, you will fall."

"Yes, Reverend Mother."

"Youth forgets easily, but I counsel you to remember my advice when you face the mirror. If you betray our bargain, there will be no place in the galaxy far away enough to hide from my retribution."

A boast I preferred not to test. "I understand."

"Mark my words. Do not give in to any temptations, however slight, against my interests. If I judge you a traitor, there will be no trial, no warning; the blade will strike you in the dark when you least expect it."

I nodded. She might kill me on a whim. I could never let my guard down.

"I will tell my sister, Lady Chani, to watch over your progress. I will too if affairs of state permit it."

23

A MATTER OF HONOR

The seneschal kept me under house arrest for the next two weeks while various functionaries administered tests, drew blood, put me through calisthenics and running regimens while hooked up to telemetry. Monitored, poked, prodded, herded and ordered about. Staff left no waking moment to me alone. They rifled through my belongings.

Nothing gratified so much as the fact that when they took all my clothing and personal effects out of my locker and inventoried them, the O-ball was not there, still buried somewhere in the Chief Steward's department..

The lesser bureaucrats could not take what they did not know existed. Palace servants in the quartermaster's guild are exacting and, while they may chance dishonesty in lesser venues, never dare to betray their lord. I had seen traces of accounting irregularities in my shop days that signalled petty theft or financial embezzlement, but no one crossed the paraman or the paramani on matters of state security.

Arkasa called on me as soon as they allowed visitors. I knew enough about sarpan tastes to offer her pickled eel.

"Delicious," she said, in Galactic. "After seeing you cross talons with a raptor, I would like to have a sample of your blood to take home for analysis."

I wore a simple white and gold tunic and trousers, bordered in green, the House colors. I sat across from her at a small cafe table arranged for our meeting. "Get in line," I said.

"A jest."

The room was barren except for archaic bookcases along one wall. A blue and gold area rug under us served as a makeshift island of civility at court for a prisoner and peon.

Arkasa growled.

"What?" I said.

"Do not get that simpering woe is me look you human youths get sometimes."

"I didn't realize I looked so pitiful," I said.

"You do not, but think yourself so. That is unbecoming of a warrior. I would like to offer you a position on my staff as an advisor on human affairs."

The offer stunned me. "Would I get to go off-world?"

"Yes, in time. Would that intrigue you?"

My family was dead. The O-ball was out of my reach. The offer of a spot at Mahara remained a wishful fantasy if I failed to earn my place once I arrived there, assuming nobles would even keep their word.

"Better," Arkasa said.

"I don't understand."

"For a moment, you looked like you might throttle a chrysanthoiguanadon with your bare hands before drinking its blood."

I understood this as a compliment, but was embarrassed that my feelings showed so.

"You have not answered me."

"I would have to think about it. Am I even free to consider the offer?"

Arkasa stood at her seven-foot height and stretched. She scratched the back of her neck with a razor-sharp talon. "I have already asked permission of the paramani should you show an interest, and she gave no answer but 'do as you will, and the boy will do as he wishes.'"

That seemed a cryptic answer to hang one's life on. I wondered what I should do. It was an agonizing dilemma. Both offers were good in their own way, with imponderable hazards, and I could not have both. Could I never find a safe choice?

Arkasa fingered the golden scroll and lightning bolt on her diplomatic badge. As intimidating as any sarpan, she was all seven feet of saurian hide and scale. Talons that could eviscerate me if she chose, herald of an empire with leaders that thought any alien flesh, sapient or not, qualified as prey for food. She was different, or she was subtle.

This only made the choice harder. What might I learn at Sarpa that could help my people, whatever the personal risk? What might I lose if I took up the offer? The paramani had given her permission, had she not?

A servant brought in a flask of water and a bowl of peeled and sliced apples. Arkasa poured me another glass of water. "Not filtrig ambervis, but alcohol is for celebrating later. What say you, Firehill?"

I took a long drink of water. What else might I gain from such a bargain? What else might I lose?

I have already struck an agreement with the paramani. Would I break it? One of the Seven Precepts forbade one to forswear or deceive. I had seen enough court politics and nobles plotting to know how little stock most humans placed in them. In the republic, bending your word for the extra gold quant, the extra measure of dominance had replaced the outdated lessons of the nursery.

What else might I lose? That settled it for me.

"I am honored, Ambassador, by the offer, but I have already given my word to the paramani, and I would not break it."

Arkasa set the glass down and stared at me with her black eyes flecked with green. "It seems you are more than just an ambitious warrior."

I bowed my head, not knowing what more could be said, so said nothing.

"Firehill," she said.

I looked back up.

"You know the rigors of my people, and judge us for it. But I say to you, the galaxy is a more dangerous place than you know, and outer space litters itself with the bones and ashes of the weak."

I could do nothing but fall back on protocol. "Yes, esteemed ambassador."

"We are jealous of our secrets, but I will teach you to speak Sarpan, if you will hazard your throat to it."

Shock and delight warred within me.

"Better. The color has come back into your face."

She bowed to me, hand across her breast in the fashion of one peer to another. "And now I must attend to my tasks, for you have another to occupy you now."

She left me alone, staring at a flask of water and the fruit on the table. I wish they had brought some meat or bread. My stomach growled. I had little time to mull over my incredulity or get over my adrenaline rush. Even friendly sarpans are intimidating, and this had been the most intimidating two weeks of my life, except for my harrowing escape from the First Sister and the death of my uncle.

I snapped out of my brooding when two palace guards in the white and gold of House Ashastra with green braided aid cords on their uniforms entered. One of the had three green slashes across a chevron marking him as a sergeant. "Kiryan Toragni ni' Ashastra," he said. "Come with us."

What now? Wearily, I stood, and they led me away.

24

THE TEST

The guards shuffled me off to the gymnasium complex. Their studied frowns and impassive stony eyes framed my world. I could not get used to my new status. At least I could bloody my fists on the makiwara board.

To my surprise, they passed me into the champion's field, the part of the complex that afflicted me with burning curiosity every time I saw those forbidden doors.

Once past the threshold, the corridors seemed no different, but I felt different and wondered what was to become of me.

They deposited me in a locker room with individual changing rooms. They engraved my name in silver on a doorplate. I did not know the other names on the other doors, but many of them had titles like admiral, general, and master of war. I suppressed the impulse to graffiti them with irreverent barbs.

They had furnished my room with multiple white training gi's, perfectly fitting and emblazoned with the wing and delta sign of Ashastra. It reminded me I was their possession, like a pet dog, and wondered if I could make myself into a wolfhound.

I exited the room in that frame of mind to meet the guards who had waited at both exits of the locker room to collect me.

"Aren't you going to tell me what your plan of the day is, soldier sir?" I said to the sergeant. He mumbled something about my cheek, and pushed me in the upper back, causing me to stumble forward.

"Just do as you are told," he said.

"I'm trying to. Why don't you tell me?"

"Follow," he said, motioning to the lead guard.

We took another path through the facility, upstairs to a solitary elevator. I balked at entering. "Where are you taking me?"

"To spar."

They refused to answer any further questions.

When we exited the elevator on a mezzanine with gallery windows looking down on the main gym, they directed me to another gymnasium as big as a football field, but instead of wood slatted floor buffed to a waxy sheen, it had another surface of ominous portent.

A broad oval space with packed dirt, a low wall ringing it. The wall appeared like bleached sandstone, exquisitely fitted blocks, yet the surfaces rugged, and it seemed weatherworn or aged.

I walked in as the elevator shut behind me. I stood in front of an altar, black as obsidian, at this end of the arena. To either side rising behind me, three tiers of low stone benches followed the arc of the place all the way to the far end, at least a furlong from me. The overall design reminded me of the gladiatorial arenas used for entertainment in most of the larger cities on Altarsha. To my right and left stood weapons racks, bearing a variety of spears, maces, halberds and pikes, and swords of every make. Short swords, rapiers, cutlasses, great two-handed swords too heavy for younger hands like mine.

The air was warm, humid, and this startled me, used to climate-controlled spaces everywhere I went. I could not see the roof of the place, or rather, it seemed like a sky made of bronze with flickering shadows in the shapes of clouds drifting slowly across it as if a high wind were blowing across the field of combat. A pungent odor of coriander or cinnamon or something in between, like incense in meditation halls, though I saw no tapers burning.

In the center stood a lone figure, a woman. She wore white and green, house colors again, in a dress that resembled my gi, but flowing, bunched up more like billows of cloud than the straight, starched fabric I wore. Her hands were folded across her chest. She extended her right hand out, palm up, and in a slow, deliberate motion beckoned me to come forth.

Scared I was. The only other places I had ever heard of, and never permitted to see while my parents were alive, were the spectacle arenas where Altarshan crowds witnessed mercenaries or condemned criminals fight in bloodied sport, sometimes to the death, but usually only to first blood. They inflicted death on criminals who were given a fool's chance to win their freedom by defeating the paraman's champion.

Here I am, I thought, my mind beseeching I knew not who. Now what? I clenched my fists at my side, unable to relax them, and strode forward until I was within ten feet of her. She extended a palm out.

She was young, perhaps in her late thirties, and her voice held the same air of authority as the paramani. "That is far enough. Let me have a look at you before we proceed," she said.

My right heel burned, the one with the tattoo. I could almost feel the dragon flying over the waves, the Fleur de lis waving like a banner above it.

Her eyes widened for a moment. She looked deliberately at my right foot, her eyelashes long and black, and she looked back up at me. She bent her right arm so her forearm faced me, and pulled back the sleeve of her fighting robe. Her skin, alabaster and without blemish, except for a shiny haze across her forearm. I squinted, focusing my attention while trying to ignore the rising heat in my heel. The haze resolved into clarity, and I beheld a tattoo of an uncoiling dragon, all serpent body, claws, fangs, bright staring eyes and smoke fuming from scaled nostrils.

"I see you, Kiryan Toragni," she said. "Though that is not the family name you were born with, it is the true one."

"How did you do that trick?" I said.

She placed her arms at her sides, the robe's sleeve concealing the tattoo. "You see what others are blind to in me. Why do you walk on your sign as if you feared discovery?

"I had no choice. With respect, who are you, and why have you brought me here?" My voice trembled.

"We must shake you out of your torpor. Too young, you have been thrown into the strife of the Great Houses, and without the preparation you should have had."

She was right. My death duel with the raptor, imprisonment, near execution and helpless confinement had rattled me worse than I thought. At the moment, the most comforting thing I could think of was to find a deep hole to hide in and curl up like a small thing of no account and just disappear. Leave me alone. What have I done to deserve your punishment?

She frowned. Her face was delicate, oval-shaped, with dark brown eyes. "Choose a weapon," she said.

"What?"

"Did you not hear my command? Choose a weapon now or fight without one."

Feeling cowed, I had no fight left in me. I trudged over to the weapons rack, which presented many archaic hand weapons: swords, spears and quarterstaffs of varying sizes and composition. A force buffeted me in my hindquarters and caused me to stumble. Chagrined,

I rubbed my ass and looked accusingly at her. "I don't know how you did that, but I am tired of being pushed around by you nobles."

She nodded. "Why then do you tarry? Choose a weapon."

I strode to the racks that had been on my left. There were no energy weapons or guns here. The one rack had polearm weapons, from quarterstaffs to pikes. No energy pikes, pity, I thought. I examined a spear, hefting it for its weight and balance. A bluff. What did I know about spear work? I jogged to the other side of the arena, glaring at my challenger as I passed before her. There were some fine swords. I thought the two-handed sword with a long curved blade with an angled tip would serve. But I knew nothing about swords. This is hopeless. Maybe I should refuse.

Something boxed my right ear. Clasping a hand to the stinging side of my head, I looked at her. She stood placidly, hands clasped across her middle, sleeves draped covering her dragon tattoo. It reminded me of mine. What game was she playing with me? A fleur-de-lis is a representation of the white lily. A dragon above the sea. What does it all mean?

Should I choose a weapon or not? Should I try to wound her or beat her? The thought was distasteful to me. Why should she be able to force me into what I was sure would be an unfair fight? I made my decision.

I walked to the center of the arena. I put my hands at my side and bowed. Then I went to a ready position, my fists clenched in front of my body center.

She arched an eyebrow. Was that a trace of amusement on her face? "What weapon will you choose, Kiryan?"

"With respect, m'lady, I choose myself."

She nodded and shed the silken robe to reveal she was wearing a uniform. Black fatigues with silver-trimmed epaulets, loose-fitting as my own gi. Her shoulder patch bore the sign of House Ashastra: a hand holding a flaming torch braced by white eagle wings, trimmed in silver on a field of green. A broad green strip of cloth from left shoulder to waist sewn into the fatigues. Rows of colored ribbons embroidered across the upper third. I had mooned after Battlefleet heroes since I was a child and knew what they meant. The highest rank was the Legion of Honor, the republic's second-highest military award. On the right side, her fatigues had a gold and silver cloth badge of the house symbol superimposed on laurel leaves with a silver star. A sign of command authority.

Incredulous. "You are the First Sister of House Ashastra."

She bowed and put her fists in front of her in the ready stance.

"Anka" Begin.

25

THE QUEEN'S CHAMPION

"What are the rules for..." I never finished the words as she did a backward spinning roundhouse kick to my jaw. Her control was that of a master. She pulled the force at the last moment. The kick stung my chin like a slap to the face instead of knocking me unconscious.

Irritated, I flowed into the forms. I remembered my training and my anger.

I never gained control of the fight. I did not recognize her style, only that I realized I had never met a true master of martial arts, not like her.

She buffeted me with a series of combination kicks and knife-hand chops. I would block the first two, then the third would strike my cheek, or my gut, and pretty soon I would be a mass of bruises.

"Your forms are passable for a beginner, Kiryan," she said. "Who taught you?"

"My father." I gasped.

She pivoted and whirled around me, a blur of black and green, her service ribbons leading my eye, the command star intimidating me. I grew faint. "Your father? And what did your mother teach you?"

The dust of the arena kicked up around me. I staggered. Gasping for air. "She taught me... songs."

"Songs? Sing me one as we fight."

She swept a foot behind mine, and a fell on my rear, humiliated.

The dragon tattoo on her forearm shimmered. Did a flame burst forth from its fanged mouth, or was that my imagination? I swear something grabbed me by my gi collar and lifted me to my feet. I stood gasping. She stepped back and folded her right fist into her left palm, arms extended.

What can I sing? I shook my head. "I have lost too much to sing for your entertainment."

"Sing of what you lost."

It was too much. "I would weep and humiliate myself further."

"Then sing and weep. It is no humiliation to mourn."

The word for war in ancient Altari is the same as the word for peace, and separated by only one word.

"Mara..." I began. Peace. That was what I lost on the day of the earthquake. My parents had pushed me hard, and I had been ungrateful. I had not reckoned they might try to prepare me for something. The words came tumbling out of me in a melody that shook my chest with the vibration. I sang of a people searching in the night and of a lost home, of taking and leaving, but I knew not what of.

Then, as the words spread their balm in my soul, they turned bitter, and in that moment, I felt the cold steel girders under my feet. It seemed my right heel vibrated with their molecules, too subtle for sound. Carbon fibers in the matrix of the vaulted ceiling tugged like spider webs pulling at my chest, tendrils of spectral energy. I took a deep breath and as I sang; I took the stalking jaguar form, right and left hands palm out, swinging arms right and left as something flowered in my chest, a heat, an anger. I saw a shimmering disk of flame in my mind's eye, and the fire, bright as a rising phoenix, filled my song.

I knew how the song ended, and when I opened my mouth; it seemed as if the breath poured out from me, magnifying the ultimate words. "Mara Ni."

They had commanded me to fight, and I looked at my opponent, singing the words. Before I could end them, she crossed both wrists in front of her face, looking past my right shoulder, eyes not meeting mine, and said the words like those that had come unbidden to me on the palace rooftop. "Ettirka Ni."

Air buffeted my left ear and spun me to the right. As I came around, I saw the obsidian table crack in two and fall into two pieces. Nauseated, I passed out.

When I woke up, I heard running water. I lay on a bamboo mat in the middle of a grotto of ferns, manicured shrubs and foliage. I wore my usual service uniform. Something or someone had washed off the grime of the arena. I swear I smelled perfume and wondered if it was me.

From behind the shadow of converging elephant ear leaves, the First Sister stepped forth. She wore the white gown of a paramani with a green and white cloak like her sister's. Sequined slippers clad her feet.

"Well, you are well, despite yourself."

"What happened back there?"

"You lost your fight."

"How could I hope to beat you? I have never seen a master of the fighting arts like you."

"That is because I am the champion of the republic. I do not speak of that."

The mist from the fountain cooled my brow. I just wanted to be left alone. "What then?"

"You lost the fight against yourself. You channeled your spirit without mastering your intentions."

This was too much. I put my face in my hands.

"Look up."

"What?"

"You learned many songs, but do not know what they mean. When you ended with Mara Ni, I was the object of your words, but I am not your enemy."

Mara Ni. To War. "The word for peace is war."

"So say some. That word would have injured another, or killed her."

I remembered the broken altar, awed. "How did you stop the effect?"

"With the negation of a negation."

I turned away, sat on my pallet, and looked down at a rock. A beetle crossed it, carapace shining from the mist.

"I have another question for you, Kiryan."

"Shoot," I said. "Not literally, please."

"Have you never wondered why with all our First Mothers, we have never had a queen? Your tattoo, like mine, is given only to champions of Great Houses."

"But I am nobody, from nowhere."

"It is not yours to choose your fate, only how you will bear it."

"I don't understand," I said.

"There is a legend that someday the queen's champion will appear."

"But you just told me the Altari have no queen."

"We do not know. Many say this is but the symbol of a perfect ruler, but some say this is a real person from a real family. That is my belief. Some call me mad for that."

"You are the Lady Chani?"

"Yes, and I will prepare you for Mahara, and to meet the ordeals that will come."

26

— • —

IF YOU WANT TO READ MORE BOOKS BY DAVID AQUINAS

1. **You can sign up for daily email newsletter updates at: https://davidaquinas.com**

Other titles by David Aquinas:

Expanding Suns ™ Book 2: *Expanding Suns — The Firehill Saga*
Expanding Suns ™ Book 3: *Under a Burning Sky*
Expanding Suns ™ Book 4: *The Mirror of Flame*

2. Also get the news on other forthcoming books in the Expanded Suns ™ universe:

The Prince of Mars, *The Return of the Prince*, and *The Queen's Guard*

And check out David's Military Science Fiction Series: *Confederation & Principate*:
beginning with the space opera romance, *Second Chance*

War, the novel that takes up the lives of two characters from the origin short story titled "If Bankers Had Space Ships"

And the forthcoming epic fantasy and fantasy romance novels titled:
A Web of Frozen Stars
A Realm of Frozen Stars and Fire

Short story anthologies from these science fiction and fantasy worlds will also be available exclusively to David's email newsletter readers, including:

Free "vanishing short stories" in the above worlds, that will be available for purchase later in the ever-expanding compendium titled *The League of Galactic Cosmic Warriors*

Email newsletter subscribers also get to see cover reveals and advance reader excerpts of future stories.

3. David brings you heroic escapist science fiction and fantasy that entertains you in a way that leaves you feeling satisfied, hopeful and inspired.

   "Enter David's Worlds and Return to Yours Refreshed and Stronger."

4. To sign up for the newsletter go to:
   https://davidaquinas.com